The Rosado Gang

Rufus Breese and gun-totin' Eady 'Britches' Dix ride north across the Rio Grande to the town of Quemadero. On their arrival, the townsfolk are suspicious and judge the pair to be connected with an infamous outlaw group that was once headed by Ida Rose. And when a powerful rancher is found dead, Rufus and Eady are arrested and thrown in jail.

Under threat from a lynch mob they must prove their innocence by fighting bushwhackers, ranchers and outlaws alike.

The Rosado Gang

Caleb Rand

A Black Horse Western

ROBERT HALE · LONDON

ISBN-10: 0-7090-8104-9
ISBN-13: 978-0-7090-8104-3

Robert Hale Limited
Clerkenwell House
Clerkenwell Green
London EC1R 0HT

Typeset by
Derek Doyle & Associates, Shaw Heath
Printed and bound in Great Britain by
Antony Rowe Limited, Wiltshire

1

A REPUTATION

In the town of Lordsburg, a miner and two land speculators destined for Silver City had waited two days for the Overland stagecoach. But a rider had brought news of trouble, and they were prepared to wait another day before going on. They voiced their fears to the driver, suggested they all go with the next coach as a combined team. It was the instinct for safety in numbers, a more effective defence against attack.

'That's yer choice gents. But I'm hired to take this ol' gal on at noon, an' that's what I'm aimin' to do,' the driver responded confidently.

There were no immediate takers for the ride, and the coach was filled with army provision boxes. There was one however, who decided to make the journey. It was a woman, and the driver suggested she fit herself inside. She was an amiable, but tough, frontier lady. Her name was Eady Dix, and she was travelling north.

It wasn't often the driver had such a mix of cargo. He considered it an obligation to mention that Rufus Breese – the hired shotgun to Fort Tyrone's stock – treat the lady with respect. One of the men who wasn't going called for Eady to rethink her journey.

'No,' she said. 'If the driver reckons he can make it, I'll take my chances.'

'Ha. She's got more sand than all o' you put together,' the driver shouted at the backs of the three departing men.

They climbed aboard the coach, Rufus Breese riding alongside the driver, Eady comfortably wedged in the pile of sacks and boxes.

The driver gathered up the reins and looked around him. 'Anyway, who'd want to stay in this Godforsaken hole?' he grumbled. Then he called out the 'Move it' ritual to his team of horses.

There were no comfortable stopping places along the route, just cold harbour relays. Between these stations, the coach rolled along at good speed, the changes usually made in less than ten minutes. At each stop, Rufus Breese got more anxious, less sure of his choice of employment. But the driver remained confident. 'We're goin' through on time,' he reassured them continuously.

'But this time, you got a lady on board,' Breese said, as he climbed back on to the riding boards.

'She ain't been pressed, an' she don't appear to be sick in the head. My money says she'll give as good as she gets.' The driver winked down at Eady, as he flicked the reins.

For two hours the coach rollicked along. The horses were enjoying the pull as they approached a shallow in Whitewater Creek, not far from the trouble spot of a week before.

'Look lively, shotgun,' the driver said loudly. 'If anythin' happens, don't talk about it . . . shoot.'

Eady poked her head out of the coach window. 'How 'bout me, driver?'

The driver looked at Breese. 'Bless her heart, she sure reminds me o' someone.'

'D'you reckon we're on our own, out here?' Rufus asked.

'Cain't tell,' the driver said thoughtfully. 'Cain't tell.'

Snake Pass was a few miles further north of the flats, on the run-in part of the journey, and ran between low rock formations winding along the side of the creek.

It was early evening as the coach slowed in its approach to the pass. Heat was still rising from the ground, but in the shimmer, mounted riders were visible from a quarter-mile out.

Breese spoke uneasily to the driver. 'There, ahead.'

The driver never flinched or took his eyes off the trail ahead. 'I seen 'em, lad. Hold tight.' He gripped the reins and sent the team into a full gallop. The coach creaked and rattled wildly in its headlong dash. The horses were fresh and strong, and they thrust their heads forward eagerly. The driver called for more effort, was cracking his whip when one of the lead pair suddenly slewed, buckled into a dive against its partner. It was fractionally after the unmistakable crack of a rifle from ahead of the coach.

Rufus and Eady were ready, and fired simultaneously, but it was into thin air. The riders had vanished into the low, layered rocks.

The dying animal had brought the coach to a halt, and the driver was staring wildly about him. He sprang from the box and ran to cut free the harness. The horse had taken a fatal bullet, its hind legs jerked, and its neck arched in its last few seconds of life.

It was then that the hold-up men reappeared from their cover. They were brandishing and firing Colts and rifles, but they held off from the coach, because Rufus and Eady were measuring out a barrage of gunfire. From huddled behind the dead horse, the driver yelled curses at the robbers and grabbed for his pistol. He flung himself low across the horse's back, emptied his cylinder into the yelling mob.

Rufus and Eady continued their fire and brought down two riders. The broken group whirled their horses, once again disappeared into the bleak landscape.

'Must have Injun blood in 'em,' Rufus rasped. 'Now cut him loose,' he yelled, grabbing up the reins again.

But the driver didn't move. He lay still and silent across the broad belly of the dead horse. The remaining horses were stamping the ground in alarm. Eady climbed from the coach, and Rufus handed her down the reins. He leaped from the box and ran with his head down. The driver had been hit twice, but wasn't yet dead.

Eady's breath was coming in short, emotional spasms as she walked up. Rufus got to his feet and took a long look at the distant hills.

'Be a while before he's up on the box again, Eady. But I reckon he'll live.' He grasped the driver by his leather jerkin, pulled him to the coach and made him as comfortable as he could across the supply boxes.

Eady cut loose the dead horse. She tied the second lead on behind, and flung the front harness on to the coach floor. Rufus was sitting ready to move off, and he looked sharply at Eady as she climbed up beside him.

'We go on,' she said and gripped the shotgun. 'I've got a thing about goin' back. Besides, there's more chance of findin' a good doctor in Silver City.'

Rufus smiled, then shook his head. 'I'm right sorry, ma'am, but I'm thinkin' you'll have to change that plan.'

The coach had been surrounded by a band of ten armed riders. Now, they'd changed their tactics, sat their horses threatening and silent.

'Goddammit!' Eady yelled. Without thinkin' she swung up the shotgun, leaped to her feet and fired both barrels out at the mounted robbers. Rufus cursed and made a grab for his Colt. The riders were stunned by the explosive retaliation, and those nearest to the coach were being whirled by their horses in fear and confusion.

Eady's hat had flown from her head, and the hold-up men caught sight of her fair, curly hair. The buck-skin coat and tight breeches only added to their confusion, their faltering return of fire. Rufus yelled, and they both rolled off the seat and swung them-selves down into the coach. They knew they weren't going anywhere and, as a great gesture of defiance, they piled more fire from the windows.

'Get the boxes around you,' he said, gently easing the driver to the floor of the coach. They lay in silence for five minutes before Rufus decided to have a look out. He squeezed himself to the other side of the coach, but there was nothing to be seen, except the rumps of the retreating horses.

'They've gone. I can see their dust.'

Eady eased herself into a corner of the coach, her feet avoiding the unconscious driver. 'How can you be sure? They ain't got nothin' yet for their pains, an' there's a brace lyin' dead. Why don't we just dig in here, an' wait for the next coach to come along?'

It was nearly dark when they heard the approach-ing coach. It was from Silver City and heading towards them. As he brought his team through the pass, the driver swerved in alongside. Without dispute, Rufus gave Eady all the credit for saving the provisions but, in the circumstances, thought it best that she travel back to Lordsburg.

The man who rode shotgun with the incoming coach, agreed to transfer, with Rufus carrying on to

Silver City with the stricken driver and the army goods.

Sitting atop the returning coach, Eady looked down as Rufus walked up. The man placed a hand on the kicking board and smiled wearily. 'A day from now, an' I'll probably see the lighter side of all that. After all – an' thanks to you, Eady Dix – no one on our team died.'

Eady nodded, smiled an acknowledgement. 'You got any other business Rufus, besides escortin' groceries for blue coats?' she asked.

'There's a small herd o' coloured stock bein' run down from Colorado. I thought I'd look me out a blood to ride north with. Maybe cross the Rio Grande.'

'Huh. I've always wanted me a smoke bayo . . . a mare. Why don't you neck me one? If I'm ridin' topsides, them bandits should let the next coach right on through. I won't be more'n a hoot an' a holler behind.'

'Yeah, I'd like that, Eady. So, maybe we could ride together,' Rufus suggested.

2

QUEMADERO

Sandwiched between the Pecos and Canadian rivers, the Rio Gargara meandered peacefully west, through sand bars and flats. Where Rufus Breese and Eady 'Britches' Dix sat shading their horses, the sedge-covered banks were dashed with seep-willow and mesquite trees.

Eady tugged at a climbing vine, smiled touchingly before flicking its blossom to the surface of the gurgling water. She held her slouch hat against the sun, squinted at the town that was hazed by the shimmer of the land ahead. 'Don't look like the sort o' place that gives trouble,' she said.

Rufus gave a quick grin. 'There was a time, you coulda said that about the road 'twixt Lordsburg an' Silver City.'

'Well, that was some other place ... some other time,' Eady said wistfully.

The patchy buildings of Quemadero lined both sides of a dog-legged street. Some clapboarded, some false-front and tented, some adobe, but all weather-beaten and baked beneath the New Mexico sun.

'What's that?' Eady asked, as they rode past a trio of deeply charred, live-oak stumps.

'That's where killers an' horse-thieves once got burned . . . how the town got named.'

'Nice,' Eady muttered, looked around for more sign of town doings.

But there was only one person in obvious sight; a tight, nervy-looking man in dust-powdered range clothes. He was standing on the boardwalk that abutted the veranda of the town's bank. Rufus had already seen him, didn't like the way he eyed them as they rode forward. There were four saddle horses close by, but they were ground-hitched, standing ready.

'There's some fellers must have a lot o' trust in their mounts,' Eady said. 'Either that or they're figurin' on goin' somewhere in a hurry. They ain't tied.'

Rufus leaned from the saddle, closer to Eady. 'That's 'cause they're robbin' the bank,' he said, out of the corner of his mouth.

'How'd you know that?' Eady asked, with a quick expectant smile.

'Can tell. Call it, bad man's eye.'

Eady brightened some more. 'We gettin' us involved?'

13

'No, we ain't. An' don't stare like that, keep ridin'.'

The two of them rode on down the street without even glancing at the man on the boardwalk. But further on, they heard a muffled shout from inside the bank building.

There was no doubting it was a distressed cry of shock. Rufus instinctively reined in his sabino, was twisting in the saddle when the hollow boom of a gunshot followed.

The man on the boardwalk stepped forward quickly. His face twisted with anger as he reached for the reins that were turned around the saddle horn of the nearest of the four horses.

'Leave them mounts,' Rufus shouted.

The man was suddenly panicked, fearful for his own hide and he made a grab for his handgun.

It was a mistake, and he howled with pain as a bullet from Rufus's long-barrelled Colt, side-swiped his right arm.

'Goddamn it, Rufe, you said to keep ridin',' Eady said, swinging her own newly acquired bayo mare in tight, testy circles.

'I'm suddenly thinkin' there might be a reward.'

'One way to get money from a bank,' Eady grunted an approval.

Troubled at the shooting, the bank-robbers' horses stomped and snuffled. Three of them found there was nothing restraining them and whirled away, went tearing down the street in a panicky gallop.

Rufus was watching them. 'Take on the gunnies,

14

Eady,' he shouted, before spurring off in close pursuit. The lookout's own horse tried to follow, but the stricken man dragged its bridle back with his good hand.

Three jittery men then dashed out of the bank. They were waving guns, probing for the expected trouble. Neck-cloths hid the lower part of their faces and their woolsey hat brims were bent down to mask their eyes. One of two men who carried a money bag, shouted furiously as he saw them retreating.

'You idiot, Vern. You've let the goddamn horses get away.'

'Yeah, an' I nearly got my goddamn arm shot off.' The lookout man named Vern, didn't try to explain further. He was having trouble enough holding on to his own mount.

At the sight of the masked men, Eady sent her mare into a few big strides to cross the street. She swung from the saddle, jumped on to the rising steps of a saloon. 'Keep still, or you could run into a bullet,' she muttered. Then she dropped the reins, and ran to duck behind a stack of empty beer barrels.

Alongside her, a big man shoved himself out through the saloon's batwing doors. He carried a Winchester, was determinedly levering a shell into the breech. He leaned back against the clapboard wall, and raised the rifle to his shoulder. He took good aim at the nearest bank robber, let out a judgemental curse and pulled the trigger.

The rifle shot bowled thunderously into the street, and the masked man was lifted backwards as the big bullet hammered into his chest. He staggered back, but didn't go over. He took a sideways step, then forward, seemed to bow for his part in the drama. Then he dropped his gun and money bag, coughed and went heavily down to the dust of the street.

The guns of the other two outlaws started a frantic retaliation. Bullets split and fractured the wall planking behind the big man and he quickly leaped to one side, joined Eady behind the barrels.

'Howdy,' Eady said. She hunkered down, let herself roll from cover. Then she raised the Colt, and fired. The robber who was carrying the other money bag, crumpled at the gunshot, tripped as he came down the bank's steps.

'They only want money. I reckon we got 'em beat,' Eady called out. But directly above her, the big man's rifle boomed again. This time the third bank raider got a bullet high in his leg. He kept going, but only to get shot again, fatally, through his chest.

Vern yelled wild and fearful as he looked towards the aggressive gunfire from across the street. He saw the rifle in the big man's hands find him. Pathetically, he raised a shattered, bloody hand, tried to voice his surrender. But it was in vain, and the rifle crashed out for a fourth and final time, caught him somewhere low and vital.

'Goddamn murderin' scum,' he hissed, before throwing himself off the edge of the boardwalk. Eady heard the man's dying words, allowed herself a short, thought-provoking moment. She stood up and, turning the cylinder of her Colt, looked along the street to where she half expected to see Rufus.

Alongside her, the big man slowly lowered his rifle. He tapped the barrel against the side of his leg, as if he was impatient for more killing.

'There's some would reckon he had a line o' reason,' Eady said, indicating the dead man.

The big man started sizing up Eady, took uncertain note of the manly garb. 'He had diddly squat,' he said glibly of the bank robber. 'An' just who the blue blazes are you?' he asked. 'This ain't work for—'

'I'm clearin' up, ain't I?' Eady snapped back fast. 'That makes it fittin' for what you had in mind. An' the name's Eady Dix.'

The man nodded good-humouredly. 'An' I'm Wheat Cater, owner o' this here Tall Top,' he said.

'Curious name,' Eady suggested.

'Family were Okies . . . millers from Chickasha. An' I got a kid brother called Rye,' Cater responded with a straight face.

'Good job they weren't meat canners. But I meant the saloon,' Eady said, similarly matter of fact.

'Oh, I see. Well, that's how they like their beer . . . them that drink here,' Cater said.

Eady saw that the saloon keeper was unsettled by her, like nearly all men, irritated. Then, the man turned away because he'd seen the gathering of a small crowd.

Eady looked down at the bodies in the street. 'Got 'emselves in the wrong line o' business,' she muttered drolly.

Cater stepped into the middle of the dusty thoroughfare, where a heavy-set man with a sheriff's badge had started to take charge. 'That's Yule Arnold,' he said, as Eady moved alongside him. 'Old-time peace-keeper from Tucumcari. He used to kick the tripes out o' you when you rode in . . . rarely on the way out.'

'Someone pick up them money bags. Take 'em back to the bank,' Sheriff Arnold rasped at the onlookers. Then he turned, looked towards the bend in the street as Rufus rode in leading the bank-robbers' horses.

'Here he comes . . . your . . .' Cater said, his eyes watching Eady for a reaction. 'I saw you ride into town together.'

'Yeah, I just bet you did,' Eady said with a thin smile, not bothering to mention a relationship.

'In this town, I watch my neighbours,' Cater said softly.

It was an obvious warning, but Eady pondered on just how Cater meant it.

'Who's wantin' these mounts?' Rufus asked, having seen the sprawled figures. 'They'll not be . . . not on the range they're ridin',' he added, a little more wistfully.

Arnold moved his penetrating look from Rufus to Eady and back again. 'Don't you two go leavin' town. I'll be wantin' a few words,' he advised. 'I'd be obliged if you could take the horses up the sheriff's office. Leave 'em at the hitch rail; I'll tend to 'em later.'

Sell 'em on as lawman's bonus, more likely, Rufus thought, doubted the reward he had in mind.

18

At that moment, Eady noticed a man in a black frock coat standing in the doorway of the bank. He had a red, jowly face, and Eady saw the jaundiced look he afforded the dead bank-robbers.

'What's *his* interest?' she asked Cater.

'Relief mainly. He's Ogden Rimsayle, owner of the Quemadero Bank. He'll give us some fittin' words.'

'You people know that Wheat Cater and me don't always see eye to eye,' Rimsayle started off in stentorian manner. 'But when it comes down to keeping what's rightly ours, I back him all the way.' The banker looked at the gathering around him, dabbed a big handkerchief at his plump features. 'Yes, folks, thanks to him, the attempt to rob the bank of our monies has been a failure.'

'It was my money I was protectin',' Cater muttered. 'Not anyone else's.'

'An' they'll be your fittin' words,' Eady muttered back.

'We got a wounded teller inside,' Rimsayle was continuing. 'But thanks to Wheat's prowess with a firearm, that's all.' Rimsayle caught Cater's eye, held up his hand in acknowledgement.

Cater raised the tip of his rifle, nodded his head in return. 'This is where I could give you a mention, Miss Dix. But I'm guessin' you ain't one for ridin' a man's due.'

'No, I'd never get away with *that*,' Eady answered back sarcastically. She had a sharp look around her, noticed how she'd caught the attention of two other men.

Cater had noticed them too. 'Barton Frimley,' he said, keeping his voice down. 'That's Clovis Finn on the left. They ain't here to make friends, that's for sure.'

'I don't see why not,' Eady laughed. 'They look the sort who've got dead enemies.'

'They ain't ever all dead,' the saloon owner said with intensity.

3

THE BARLEY PARCEL

With their curiosity only partly satisfied, the small crowd reluctantly drifted away. But Eady noticed that the two men Wheat Cater had identified were quicker to leave.

Yule Arnold asked for the bodies of the four bank-robbers to be carried to the livery stable to await burial. The town had its own grave patch, a mile out of town in a fork of the Gargara.

Rufus was watering his sabino at the trough, and Eady collected her own mount. It was where she'd left it, out front of the saloon, long-suffering with its reins still brushing the dust. The pair eased their saddles and led the horses further along the street, tied them to the hitch opposite the bank.

21

The sheriff stepped out from where he'd been asking questions of the wounded teller. He looked full of himself, believed the town should be thankful for his safeguarding.

'I'm Yule Arnold. An' that's givin' you the advantage,' he called out. 'Not somethin' I'm normally strong on.'

'Sheriff,' Rufus countered 'I'm Rufus Breese, an' this here's Eady Dix. We're crackin' a jar. You want some?'

'Yeah, but I'll buy,' Arnold offered. 'Call it a small reward.'

'Didn't know there was another sort,' Eady muttered, as the three of them passed under the Tall Top's overhang. The sheriff led through the batwings to where it was shadier, but no cooler.

There was no sign of Wheat Cater, only a handful of customers besides the barkeep. Clovis Finn was sitting alone at a table, skilfully riffling a deck of cards. The man named Frimley was drinking at the far end of the bar. Finn was dressed plain, somewhere between town and country. Barton Frimley was wearing a tight-fitting, black suit. They didn't appear much concerned by the sheriff, but Eady knew that she and Rufus had already been marked out as further trouble.

Eady was wondering how safe it was to stand ground between Finn and Frimley. 'Give me leopard sweat an' lemonade sumac . . . separate glasses,' she said to the barkeep.

The man pulled a brown glass bottle from a shelf,

hooked the top off and pushed it towards Eady. 'You don't get a glass with that,' he said.

'I'll take the bottle,' Rufus told him with regard to the cheap whiskey.

'You'll not,' Arnold said. 'It's sheriff's reserve for me an' my friends,' he advised the barkeep.

From along the bar, Frimley turned and stared at the banter. Eady downed her sweet, cloudy brew in a long pull, licked her lips and stared back. Frimley recognized the dash of challenge, and for a moment was disconcerted. If it had been a cowboy, he would have made something of it. But this was different, outside of his grasp, so he turned and walked nonchalantly from the saloon.

Eady was pleased at how she'd fared, but guessed it wasn't good for anything in the long term. Ah, what the hell, she thought, and exchanged a mischievous smile with Rufus.

The two other men, who still didn't appear to be too interested in the presence of the sheriff, made their way over to Finn's table.

'That couple's from the Barley Parcel. They work for Frimley,' Arnold informed Rufus and Eady.

Eady frowned with curiosity. 'Barley Parcel?' she enquired. Sounds like some sort o' Thanksgivin' box. What is it with names in this town?'

Arnold shrugged. 'It's the top an' tail of his name. He got it tagged onto what was originally a parcel o' free government land.'

The barkeep, who was always interested in the brew of trouble, decided to chip in. 'That feller Vern, who was hangin' on to the horses, he tied in with Frimley, about a week ago. That's short, even for seasonal work,' he reflected, meanly.

'It sure gives him a longer time dead. If I had any lawful muscle, I'd be checkin' the whys an' where-fores o' that,' Rufus said.

'Well, you ain't,' Arnold said bluntly.

'Yeah, that's true,' Eady said.

'See you sometime, Sheriff.' Deliberately, Rufus tossed a silver dollar on to the counter to pay for the drinks.

The sheriff sniffed indifferently, offered up his glass for more whiskey, as Rufus and Eady turned their backs on the bar.

Outside of the saloon, Eady waved her hand against the oppressive heat. 'Be interestin' to know who the sheriff's sidin' with,' she said.

'I'd've thought that was plain,' Rufus answered.

Eady shook her head. 'Most lawmen play cards tight to their bellies. He's no different. Any or either way, Rufe, there's some grain to peck hereabouts.'

Rufus and Eady didn't move straight along. Their attention had been drawn to three riders who were advancing from the other end of the street.

The man on the left was bean-pole thin, carried a white moustache that waterfalled his mouth. He rode with an authority that clearly reached well in to the town.

'He's got to be somebody,' Eady said, measured and thoughtful.

24

'Yeah,' Rufus agreed, noticing the quality of the horses the men were riding. 'They ain't ridin' buzzard bait.' He glanced the other way, along the street. 'Here comes your friend, the filler o' bone-yards. Ask him, why don't you?'

Wheat Cater nodded in acknowledgement as he reached the boardwalk. He took a step up, then turned and spoke out. 'You ought to get that foreman o' yours buttoned,' he growled at the moustachioed old rider. 'I don't take to bein' rail-roaded.'

'I'm sorry, Yule,' Emile Rednapp answered back. 'He don't mean any harm. Not normally.' Stub Jessel, the man Rednapp was referring to, snorted contempt. The third rider, a younger, flat-featured man, stared at Emile Rednapp agitatedly.

'Ain't many get a "sorry" from you, Pa,' he said.

'Wheat an' me are old friends,' Rednapp said quickly.

'Yeah, bosom buddies, I bet,' Eady said out of the side of her mouth. It was just as she turned away, that she saw the steel glint from a rooftop on the opposite side of the street. Eady saw the sharp, dark features plain behind the sights of the rifle. In one move-ment, she stepped sideways, got support from a timber column, and made an instinctive move for her high-holstered Colt. Within seconds she'd fired off three shots, waited another to see if she'd need a fourth. A fasciaboard at the top of the false-fronted building was holed, broken where her bullets had smashed a way through.

'Jeeesus!' Rufus exclaimed. 'This sure ain't any of dog town.'

The moment that Eady had moved, she and Rufus were covered by the guns of the three incoming riders. The men had reacted instantly, with the thought that it was them that Eady had been gunning for.

Eady swore. But it was with some relief, because she noticed that Cater was without his Winchester. The gun that had been fired earlier with such deadly effect was lying on the handrail fronting the saloon's veranda.

'What the hell game you playin', lady?' Emile Rednapp's voice lashed out at Eady. 'We in the middle o' some goddamn vaudeville show?'

'Him up there ain't,' Eady responded, with a nod at the roof opposite.

'You go find out what Mrs Sharp-shooter's talkin' about, Stub,' Rednapp directed Stub Jessel. 'Remember, if there *was* someone up there, he'll be of sour temper.'

'Oh, he's still up there,' Eady said, the certainty quite clear in her voice.

Jessel swung his horse across the street. He dismounted, looped the reins around the horn of the saddle.

The hinges of a batwing squeaked, and everyone turned to see the sheriff step from the saloon. He was still holding the cards from his game of poker. 'Now what?' he demanded gruffly.

'Better late than not at all, eh, Sheriff?' Rufus said,

before Arnold had a chance to speak further.

Eady was reloading her Colt. 'Must be a long time since Tucumcari,' she added cuttingly.

4

ROSADO

From high on the building, Stub Jessel looked down to the street. 'Don't know him, boss,' he called out to Emile Rednapp. 'Looks like a chilli.'

'Who shot him?' Yule Arnold's tone was curt.

'I did,' Eady said. 'He was lookin' to drop one of us, here. Didn't seem a fair contest.'

'Welcome to the town where nothin' much ever *is*,' growled the sheriff.

Rednapp and his son swung down from their saddles, fastened their reins to the rail out front of the saloon. Emile Rednapp strode over to Eady and offered his hand.

'Looks like I owe you, ma'am,' he said. 'My name's Emile Rednapp. My ranch is the Ancho Arena. I may've been wrong about the show, but not about the quality o' your gun work. If you're lookin' for any, I'd like to make first offer.'

'Yeah, that goes for me too,' Max Rednapp said. 'What's your name?'

'Eady Dix,' Eady said. 'This is my partner Rufus Breese. Lucky I happened to look up, I guess.'

'Yeah, an' I'm wonderin' who's loco enough to ambush me in broad daylight,' Rednapp senior said.

'Who *was*,' Wheat Cater laughed. Then he picked up his rifle and walked into his saloon.

Stub Jessel got back to the street. He picked out Eady, and made straight for her. 'For a ma'am, you shoot good,' he commended. 'Two o' them bullets were set closer than the feller's black eyes. So, I'd say you ain't no real ma'am.'

Eady took a deep breath, but before she answered, Rednapp was introducing Jessel. 'Stub's my fore-man,' he said. 'He's paid to get to trouble before it gets to me.'

Eady smiled patiently, watched Jessel hand some-thing to Rednapp.

'He had *this* around his arm,' the Ancho Arena foreman, said.

Rednapp sucked air sharply through his teeth, turned a shade paler. 'A pink garter,' he said, then thought for a long few seconds. 'I thought the days o' the Rosado were over. Includin' Ida Rose.'

Stub Jessel looked from Max to his father. 'Thinkin's far from knowin',' he muttered, squinting back up at the roof top.

'Nearly lost track o' what we came into town for, Max,' Rednapp said, shaking his head, seeking escape from his train of thought. 'Let's you an' me go buy us some commodities ... some goddamn comforts too.'

Max still appeared to be troubled as he followed his father. Jessel had a quick glance at Eady who gave a 'see you' nod towards Rednapp.

'I'll get the body brought down. Wouldn't want it botherin' anyone,' Arnold said testily.

Rufus stepped closer to Eady. 'What the hell was so worryin' about that scrap o' fumadiddle?' he asked quietly.

'I really can't think, Rufe. But Rednapp went a tad balky, when he saw it,' Eady replied. 'Findin' out could be interestin'.'

'Well, I think we should ride on.'

'Hmm, perhaps we should,' Eady said with a small smile. 'But not before sun up.'

Rufus made a move towards their horses. 'I don't think *this* is the place I meant to get to,' he muttered.

Eady moved alongside. 'It's kind o' weird, though,' she said. 'Who, an' what the hell's Rosado? Don't *you* think it's curious, Rufe?'

Rufus grabbed at his sabino's bridle. 'Not really,' he affirmed. 'Might if I was stayin', but I ain't. Let's get our horses put away ... go look for some food an' lodgin'.'

'I'da thought we were too far from the Cristos, for mountain goat,' Rufus said.

The stable owner spat, dribbled dark juice down the front of his hickory vest. He grinned a mouthful of dirt-rooted stubs. 'Thought I'd be seein' you two sooner or later,' he rattled. 'Pentland Betts don't miss much that goes on in this town.'

'Good. So, you won'ta missed the least worst place to stay,' Rufus said amicably. 'We're puttin' up for the night.'

The man grinned, his face squeezing into deep creases. 'That'll be the Longfield, right on down the street,' he said. 'You can't miss the place. It's got windows you can almost see through.'

Rufus nodded his thanks. 'We'll say it was recommended.'

When Rufus and Eady entered the double-fronted lodging house, it wasn't as bad as they expected. There were comfortable looking chairs, the dust was no more than a few days old, and once-bright curtains were drawn to the sides of its windows.

'Welcome,' said the slim, raven-haired girl who stood watching them from behind a reception desk. 'I'm Beth Longfield.'

'Howdy,' Eady said. 'We been told you could find us a couple o' rooms.'

The girl smiled. 'Mr Betts tells everyone that. He's on a cut for gettin' 'em booked out.'

Eady saw her look to one side, past her towards the door that had opened. She turned to see who had removed the hospitable smile.

The plain-dressed man who came in was one of the very few Quemadero folk that Eady would have recognized.

Clovis Finn removed his hat, fixed his eyes on the girl. 'That Mex who was gunnin' for Rednapp? He

31

was carryin' a pink garter,' he told her. Finn ignored Eady and Rufus, although he'd allowed them a sharp glance. 'I just heard about it in Cater's place,' he continued. 'So, they're talkin' of Ida Rose.'

'Oh no,' Beth shuddered, and let go of the dipping pen she'd picked up. 'That can't be, Clovis.'

'It sure ain't best news, if it is,' Finn said dourly. 'I thought you'd want to know.'

Beth remembered that Eady and Rufus were waiting. They were still standing close and couldn't help but overhear. She turned to them, her eyes suddenly searching for any nuance of association.

'Sorry about that,' she said, offering Eady two keys. 'One's a corner room, looks over the street. There's hot food at eight.'

5

DEAD TO THE WORLD

Eady knew that Clovis Finn was watching her and Rufus. The man whom Wheat Cater said wasn't there to make friends, was leaning against the desk. He suddenly appeared to be interested and took a couple of steps towards them.

'Whoa! Just hold up a moment,' he called out.

Eady exchanged a wary look with Rufus as they stopped and turned.

'You talkin' to us, or's there a mule just come through the door?' Rufus asked.

Finn was unperturbed. 'You ridin' on, or aimin' to stick around?' he asked.

'We ain't made up our minds just yet. Either way it ain't your business,' Rufus told him.

'Yeah, unless you're thinkin' o' makin' it so,' Eady

matched Rufus's irritation.

'No. I've seen you two out there in the street. But if not me, there'll be *somebody* interested in what your plans are.'

Rufus eyed the man with a testing glare. 'Well, it can only be a friend o' that bushwhacker. Let *them* do the askin',' he retorted coldly.

'I didn't mean any trouble. An' I'm sure Beth don't want any of it.'

Rufus and Eady watched as Finn tipped the brim of his hat to Beth Longfield. As he left, Eady was going to say that they didn't ride into Quemadero to make trouble. But she knew that was their business, and didn't.

She went on up the stairs and, after a long suspicious look behind him, Rufus followed. They trod well-worn carpeting to their rooms where Eady put the key into the lock.

'You think he was tryin' to warn us off,' Rufus asked.

'Yeah, I do think. An' it's got me even more interested in what the hell's goin' on around here.'

'I think we should've rode on through . . . headed for somewhere else,' Rufus muttered.

Eady turned the key and pushed the door open. 'An' this ain't goin' to change your mind,' she said, staring down at the man who was spread-eagled on the floor. 'One of us has got a room with a goddamn stiff already checked in.'

Rufus hissed a thin sound of astonishment as he moved past Eady into the room. 'He's doin' more than sleepin' somethin' off,' Rufus said, kneeling beside the body. The ornate handle of a parasol stick was protruding from the dead man's lower belly. A pink, satin garter was stretched tight around his neck.

'Must've come as a surprise. Whoever he is, he never got to pull his gun,' Eady pointed out.

Rufus looked up, saw the door of the room quietly closing. 'Eady,' he called out. 'Someone's closin' the door.'

Behind Eady, the door pulled to. The key clicked, quickly turned the lock in its housing.

Eady turned and made a futile pull at the handle. 'Too late, Rufe. Someone's got us corralled.'

'If it ain't Miss Longfield, it's Finn . . . got to be,' Rufus said. 'But what the hell for?'

'I can think of what the sheriff'll stick us with, if we stay,' Eady reasoned.

Rufus grunted out an agreement, moved to face the door. He considered for a very short moment, then drove the heel of his boot solidly against the stile. The wood cracked loudly and gave way, half of the door immediately breaking open. 'So let's get out,' he said, drawing his Colt.

But Eady held up her hand. She quickly rifled through the dead man's clothing, eased her fingers into a blood-dampened pants pocket. 'Just curious to know who we're supposed to have killed?' she stated. She withdrew a folded envelope, opened it out and read the address: *Speke Dancer. Stones Ranch. c/o Quemadero Cattle Office. New Mexico.*

Rufus stepped back cautiously from the landing

into the open doorway.

'If he *is* Speke Dancer, he won't mind me readin' this,' Eady said.

> *Dear Speke*
> *Remember our leaving present for them Rosados?*
> *Remember Ida Rose high-kicking into her grave?*
> *Perhaps you remember her saying she'd hunt us like*
> *dogs. Well, looks like she has, Speke. So you keep*
> *watchful.*
> *Your old friend, July T.*

'Huh. I guess he shoulda heeded his own advice,' Rufus said. 'Is all o' this feedin' that inquisitive streak o' yours, Eady?'

'Takin' the edge off an appetite maybe,' Eady flipped back. 'You know, before we leave town, we got to find out who riddled this poor feller.'

'There ain't no *got to* about it. But I know it's what we're goin' to do.'

'We got no choice, Rufe. We're caught up. If we ride out now, we won't be ridin' free.' Eady shoved the letter into her own pants pocket. She dragged the stretched garter from the man's neck over his head. She frowned and looked at it closely. Then she put that too, in her pocket. 'Let's just get out of here before someone turns up,' Rufus said.

They both walked back down to Beth Longfield's desk casually. She was talking to a weather-beaten old man who was rumbling on about the coach from Quemadero.

'Nah, I won't be needed for much longer,' he drawled. 'The railroad's goin' to run a spur line, east-bound from Albuquerque.'

'I wouldn't worry yourself about that, Enoch,' Beth said. 'By the time that happens, we'll all be restin' real quiet.'

Eady put the room keys on the desk top. 'Seems like there's *some body* in one of our rooms. Couldn't disturb 'em, they're just dead to the world,' she said calmly, and with a straight face. Beth Longfield looked surprised. 'I'm sorry. I don't know how that could have happened. I've got two empty rooms, but they overlook the trash cans. I really am sorry, I—'

'They'll do just fine,' Eady said hurriedly. She thought that Beth looked fittingly surprised. If she knew there was a body upstairs, it was a good response.

'You'll see them. There's no numbers on the back rooms,' Beth said.

'I was just wonderin',' Rufus said casually, as Eady took the new keys. 'A while back, we met up with a feller named Speke Dancer. He said he'd find us work if we wanted. Perhaps you've heard o' him?'

'Why of course. Most people on the Gargara know Mr Dancer. He owns the Stones Ranch. In fact, he was here last night. He left us this morning though . . . first light, apparently.'

'Yeah, he left us all right,' Eady said softly.

A quizzical look passed across Beth's face. 'How do you mean?' she asked.

'She don't mean nothin',' Rufus said, with a quick,

37

stuttering laugh. 'She's scratchy at us not findin' the right work. Thinks legitimate employers are avoidin' us, for some reason.'

Beth looked a little perturbed, smiled uncertainly as Rufus squeezed Eady's shoulder.

6

THE GUILT

Talking seriously, Yule Arnold, Barton Frimley and Wheat Cater strode into the Longfield. Rufus and Eady were standing with their backs against the reception desk. They held disguised interest, as the three men walked up to them.

'Looks like we quit the scene in time,' Rufus muttered, out of the side of his mouth.

'So, what have you done with him?' Arnold demanded.

'That some sort o' riddle?' Rufus enquired, against the sheriff's aggressive manner.

'I hear one o' you two's just done in Spekman Dancer. So don't mess with me,' the sheriff retorted.

'They've only just arrived here, Sheriff,' Beth explained quickly. 'And Mr Dancer's not here. There's only Clovis Finn been in. He came to tell me about—'

39

'The Rosado,' Frimley intervened. 'Yeah, we reckon they're ridin' again, Beth. It was Clovis told us about Speke Dancer.'

'Defamin' ain't lawful, even in these godforsaken parts, Sheriff. So, perhaps you better listen to what we got to say,' Rufus addressed himself to Yule Arnold.

Arnold gave an almost imperceptible nod. 'Say what you got to,' he said.

'The body's in one o' the rooms Miss Beth gave us the keys to,' Rufus answered. He glanced at Beth, who gasped audibly. 'He's been stabbed, but it weren't with no knife.'

'But Mr Dancer left early this morning,' Beth stuttered, the blood draining from her face.

'No, he ain't been nowhere, not in that state,' Rufus said, looking again at the sheriff. 'We heard the name Ida Rose mentioned once or twice. That floats in the pot, does it?'

'Who the hell you been talkin' to, mister?' Wheat Cater demanded.

'That name means somethin' to you folk . . . this town then?' Rufus asked bluntly.

'At best, Ida Rose was a horse-thief. At worst . . . well, we don't want to get into that, not in front o' Miss Beth.'

'Just pretend I'm not here,' Eady muttered, as Cater went on.

'Last fall, Ida Rose got herself strung up. I remember her last words, like most of us do. She said she'd be seein' us again. We weren't to sleep too deep.'

'From hereabouts, was she?' Eady asked Arnold.

'Yeah. She ran her line o' business from the end o' town. But there was some got their laces straightened, an' routed her an' her girls . . . burned their tent city. Ida took rare bad exception. Them Rosados turned feral, joined up with some bad Chicanos, a few renegade Comanche. Those that got a look, said you couldn't tell 'em apart.'

'Why didn't you set fire to 'em at the oak stumps?' Eady asked scornfully.

Arnold meant to respond but changed his mind. 'I knew no good would come o' that night,' he said. 'There was no law against much o' what they did . . . still ain't.'

'My pa was there,' Beth put in. 'He had to live with knowing there wasn't much guilt. Huh, it was Thanksgiving, too.'

The sheriff turned to Frimley. 'I'm curious as to why Finn should be pokin' his nose in,' he said. Then he spoke to Rufus. 'Wheat asked who it was you'd been talkin' to.'

'No one.' Eady pulled Speke Dancer's note from her pants pocket. 'I took this . . . thought we might need it, if things got unhealthy.'

While Arnold ran his eye over the note from July T, Eady told of what happened after she and Rufus had checked in.

'You said there was someone asleep,' Beth said, noticeably confused.

'Sorry, I never did. I was just smart-mouthin',' Eady responded, with an uncomfortable smile. 'But

41

we thought you could have set us up.'

'You don't know she didn't,' Arnold said.

'The lady told us the man left early. We believed her,' Eady said.

'Go an' speak with whoever it was told her otherwise,' Rufus suggested.

'Oh, I'm goin' to,'Arnold muttered. Then he thought for a moment, and handed the note to Cater. He looked from Eady to Rufus. 'The man who wrote that's July Tomkiss,' he explained. 'He used to be Speke Dancer's foreman at Stones Ranch.'

Cater looked up and shuddered. 'Looks like we do have the ghost of a goddamn hurdy-gurdy girl comin' after us.'

'That's claptrap. I'm takin' a look upstairs,' Arnold said. 'You comin', Wheat?'

'No. I'll give these two the low-down on Ida Rose and her gang. They've a claim on knowin'.'

'I think I should have gone up with the sheriff,' Beth said to Eady. 'Did you relock the door?'

'No,' Rufus started, then he shrugged. 'We thought it best left open.'

'Who exactly is this Ida Rose? Why's she causin' such a stir?' Eady asked Cater.

'That's what I was goin' to tell you. It's an unusual story. The line girls were part o' the Quemadero fixin's for a few years. They came west, then south with the silver miners after '49. They mostly kept to 'emselves . . . ploughed their earnin's back into the town. Manure, someone called it. Ida Rose was their leader, their *madam*, a woman o' name an' fame.

42

Then, about a year ago, a big dose o' respectability blew in from the East. You've sort o' picked up on the rest o' the story.'

'Yeah, it's an unusual one,' Rufus observed. 'But, as the sheriff said, it don't rightly put 'em outside o' the law. Where'd they go?'

'North end o' the Conchas Lake, apparently,' Cater said. 'It makes sense. Someone I know upriver, says he's got a supply o' horses. Most of 'em are branded, but he don't ask too many questions o' *comancheros*. He pays bedrock dollar, as they run.'

'An' that's how you tie in Ida Rose and the rest of her gang?'

'Most have. In these parts, I guess they all look like some sort o' grubby dove.'

'An' they're runnin' stock from here?'

'Yeah. Between here an' the Canadian, there's four ranches. Lyman Hench's Twisted G horse ranch, an' Emile Rednapp's Ancho Arena. There's Frimley at Barley Parcel, an' Speke Dancer's got the Stones. It was a long summer last year, an' they was all losin' stuff.'

'Frimley too?' Rufus queried.

'Yeah. Why?'

'Maybe it explains why he was so wayward with his suspicions. He's also got some leerylookin' 'punchers.'

Cater was about to continue with the story, when an excited youth bumped his way through the front door.

'I got to find the sheriff,' he gasped. 'They said

he'd be here.'

'He is. What's the problem, kid?' Cater said.

'Big trouble, Mr Cater,' the boy went on hurriedly. 'We got caught by the horse-thieves. They rode in this mornin' . . . had their faces all hid. They shot one of our boys, an' set fire to the hay barn. They stole the saddle-brokes we were drivin' up to Raton. I got to tell the sheriff.'

'You just did, Oggie,' Arnold called out, as he came back down the stairs with Barton Frimley and Beth Longfield close behind him.

'Mr Hench is steamin', Sheriff. He said I was to bring you fast as I could.'

'I think he meant as fast as *I* could. He'll have to live on the difference,' Arnold retorted, and hitched up his broad gunbelt.

'They sound like the Comanche raiders of old,' Cater said, agitated and plainly nervous. 'There was a time when they'da come with ghost shirts pulled over their wicked heads. Perhaps Ida Rose an' her girls *have* got back with 'em.'

Eady was thinking that Cater's response was irrational. How could a man who'd stood his ground to gun down a gang of bank-robbers, be quite so fearful of the alleged Rosada Gang?

7

SHADOW OF A DOUBT

Soon after hearing young Oggie's story, Yule Arnold got himself a bunch of riders together. Eady and Rufus, Wheat Cater and Barton Frimley were among those who rode with him to the Hench ranch.

'I wasn't one of them who tried to stretch her neck. Why should Ida Rose come for me?' demanded Lyman Hench. 'You reckon these goddamn Rosados are plannin' to kill or maim everythin' twixt the Pecos an' the Canadian 'cause o' that lynch mob?'

'I don't rightly know,' Arnold replied 'But I got more'n a hunch we're in for trouble.'

'You rode out here to tell me we're in for *trouble*?' barked Hench. 'How many cattle, horses an' men you lost, Sheriff?'

'I came to tell you, we're goin' after 'em,' Arnold

45

said, taking up the sting of Hench's wrath. 'An' this time, the job'll be done right. We'll bring 'em in.'

It was early dusk when the sheriff spurred his horse away from the ranch. He looked purposeful, but after two hours, Rufus suspected that he might not be too certain as to where he was riding – where they were *all* riding.

'Pretty soon, we'll be ridin' into our own dirt,' he said to Eady.

Wheat Cater overheard, and had the same idea. 'Admit it, Yule,' he grumbled. 'There ain't no trail, an' you don't really think they're headed back to Conchas Lake, do you?'

'So where else are they goin'? Arnold rasped back.

When the other riders sided with Cater, the sheriff reluctantly agreed to head back. The unofficial and makeshift posse gave each other a thankful look. In the near full dark, they turned their horses to Quemadero.

When Eady and Rufus walked into the Longfield dining-room, it was late, but the evening meal was still under way. Frimley and two of his men were already seated at one table. Cater and Finn were at another, on the opposite side of the room.

'You know what, Eady?' Rufus said. 'I got me a desire to do Clovis Finn some harm. It was *him* put the word out, that it was us killed Dancer.'

'We don't know that for certain, Rufe,' Eady said quietly. 'Frimley could have been lyin'.'

'Yeah, could have been,' Rufus agreed, sought

confirmation by looking across at the Barley Parcel rancher.

They took a table in the near corner. Rufus noticed the butt of Eady's Colt, felt safe enough to sit with his back to the room.

'Arnold ain't a hostile any more,' Eady said. 'I talked to him when we were ridin' back to town. He knows we didn't kill Dancer.'

'An' how'd he know that?'

'The man was stiff. If he'd been any stiffer, he'd've broke in two, that's how. He'd been dead since early mornin'.'

'Did Arnold ask why Beth said that Dancer had checked out at first light?'

'I don't think he had time to before we rode to Hench's,' Eady said. 'It must've been the night clerk, who told her that. Who else would have known?'

Across the room, Frimley rose from his table. He walked ominously to where Rufus and Eady were sitting. 'You two are gettin' to bite my ass,' he said testily, and gripped the butt of his gun for leverage. 'If either o' you got somethin' on your mind, spit it out.'

Eady made a low, disrespectful noise, but sat motionless. She sensed that this time there'd be no indulgent smile to share with Rufus.

Frimley's face clouded heavy when, once again, there was no impulsive retaliation from Eady.

'That's no way to address a lady an' gentleman of peace an' breedin',' was Rufus's timely suggestion. 'You certainly are a boorish, bad-mannered son-of-a-bitch, mister. Furthermore, I'll look an' talk to anybody I choose.'

At that, Frimley grabbed a fistful of Rufus's collar and dragged him up from his chair. But Rufus was ready. He'd known the move was coming, had contributed to it. In a moment, the heel of his boot was crunching into Frimley's toes. He twisted his body and bunched the knuckles of his right fist sharply into the side of Frimley's face. Then, with a short left, he hit him low and very hard in the belly.

Rufus stepped back as Frimley crumpled slowly at his feet, at Beth Longfield's timely appearance in the dining-room doorway.

'You put that devilish thing away,' she snapped at Eady, who'd got her Colt levelled across the room at Frimley's table.

Then, Frimley scrambled to his feet. He was incensed, clogged with anger, and half his face was already swollen and red-blotched.

'This sort o' behaviour could give your place a bad name,' Rufus said, with a tired grin.

'It's certainly the sort of behaviour best kept for the trash yard, Mr Breese,' Beth reproved. 'There wasn't much evidence of that gentleman you mentioned.'

'I'm sorry, ma'am. But we mustn't let it spoil the moment,' Rufus grinned apologetically. Eady coughed, and thrust her gun back in her holster.

'It was Frimley did the callin', Beth,' Wheat Cater, called out, and then laughed. 'He sure ain't a student o'nature.'

Rufus flexed his fingers, looked down at the

checkered tablecloth and shiny cutlery. 'I ain't even got to see the puddin' list,' he said as he reseated himself.

One of Frimley's cowboys took his hat from the rack. He handed Frimley his, and all three Barley Parcel men headed for the door.

Eady watched them leave, then she got to her feet. 'We're truly sorry, ma'am,' she said. 'But Mr Breese just had to defend the honour of all us girls, don't you think?'

Beth gave the pair a doubtful look, but her displeasure had faded. Then she turned and walked from the room.

Eady sat down again, kept her eye on Clovis Finn when he followed Beth. She'd already noticed that Beth held more than a passing interest in the card player. For some irrational reason, she thought that Rufus wasn't approving.

A half-hour later, Wheat Cater went to pay for his meal. He stopped and looked at Eady and Rufus as he made to pass their table.

'I don't fancy your chances. Not when he's attackin' peach cobbler,' Eady said of Rufus as he turned his spoon into the deep fruit filling.

'No, nor do I,' Cater smiled. 'Do you mind if I sit a moment? I won't disturb your meal.'

Rufus nodded that it was OK, and Cater got himself a chair and sat down.

'It weren't Clovis Finn that accused you o' killin' Speke Dancer. He's just told me he didn't even know about it. Frimley was lyin'. That's maybe somethin' else you should know.'

'Yeah, but I'm sure it don't surprise us,' Eady said indifferently.

As Eady spoke, she looked beyond Cater. She saw the shadowy figure who'd appeared in the doorway, and weird unease made her tremble. It was a tall woman of slight build, her ash-coloured hair falling in long sheaves either side of a ribboned shirt. She stood very still, her piercing blue eyes holding Eady's for a moment as she quartered the room. Then, as ephemerally as she'd appeared, she turned and was gone.

Eady organized her thoughts for a moment. 'This Ida Rose, we been chasin'; she'd have to be suntouched to ever ride back into Quemadero,' she suggested.

Cater nodded keenly at the idea. 'Ida was a big passel o' things, but plum stupid weren't ever one of 'em,' he said. 'Anyways, in her cadaverous state, she'd be smelled out before she crossed the Rio Gargara.'

Eady curled her lip with distaste. 'I wonder,' she speculated.

'Well, I got to get goin'.' Cater gave Eady a baffled look, then pulled on his Stetson. 'There's business at High Top needs takin' care of.'

Rufus looked up from the last of his meal, and Cater acknowledged him as he walked from the room. Outside, he hesitated on the raised boardwalk and savoured the night air. He flexed his shoulders and gave a thin smile, strode on briskly towards his saloon.

'There's somethin' I just got to tell you, Rufe,' Eady was telling Rufus. 'An' I hope Miss Longfield's servin' somethin' stronger than coffee.'

8

DELEGATION

When Eady and Rufus had eventually finished their meal, deliberated recent events and likely outcomes, the Longfield appeared to be deserted. There was no sign of Clovis Finn and Beth, or of the stranger whose identity Eady had more than speculated on.

'You still got them other room keys?' Rufus asked.

'I have, an' I'm gettin' mighty close to usin' one of 'em. I wonder if the sheriff got to question the night clerk?'

'Oh, who cares,' Rufus muttered. 'Right now, I'm busted too.'

They didn't see or hear anyone as they made it to the upstairs landing. Rufus took the keys, and unlocked the door. He lit a lamp and looked around the room.

'Anyone in there?' he called out a moment later.

'Only me,' Eady answered, looking back from the adjoining room.

*

Rufus and Eady had been more than an hour into their sleep, when a band of horsemen approached the Rio Gargara. They'd ridden hard, circled places where tight thickets of ocotillo choked a through route.

At the head of the line, their leader held up his hand to signal a halt. 'Remember, first four's headin' for Quemadero. Follow the river, an' wait for the signal,' he ordered.

'What about the rest of us,' one of the others asked, as the column bunched.

'You're with me, headin' for the Ancho Arena,' the leader told him. 'Rednapp's got a herd for the rail-head. They're headin' out at first light. I've got somethin' special for you, Nate,' he added.

'What's that then, boss?' the man who was named Nathan Greensleeves, asked. 'Somethin' more fillin'?'

'To your way o' thinkin', yeah. A couple o' plants need diggin' in.'

'Ha, that's better,' Greensleeves said confidently. 'Who are they?'

'They're called Rufus Breese an' Eady Dix. Makes no difference one of 'em bein' a woman – not if she's got a Colt in her paw. They're put up at Longfield's.'

'I've heard of 'em. It's her that brought down the pepper gut, this mornin'. Yeah, she's *some* sharpshooter.' Suddenly, Greensleeves didn't sound quite so sure of himself.

'You sure you're up to it? Tell me now if you ain't.'

'I ain't lived this long by not bein' appreciative of a fair gun, boss. Just means takin' more caution.'

The boss man scrutinized him. 'Well, make sure that ain't more'n two days,' he insisted.

Nathan Greesleeves raised his hand in response, swerved his horse across the water towards Quemadero.

Out on the Ancho Arena, the lone nighthawk was murmuring a few words from 'Git Along, Little Dogies', as he circled the bedded-down herd. The weary cowboy didn't see the shadowy, dark-skinned figure that appeared from the stand of mesquite, or the glint of moonlight on the blade of a skinner's knife.

'You git *yourself* along,' the rustler mocked, as he sprang silently. The fingers of his left hand dug into the rider's neck, his right plunged the knife deep into the man's side.

The dying man's song broke into a stuttering gasp as he slid from the saddle, twisted heavily into the hard ground.

The rustler gave a sharp whistle, and almost instantly, horsemen emerged from the darkness to surround the herd.

'Get the horse,' the boss man called as loud as he dared. 'If it gets back, they'll send out guns.' A rider kicked his horse after the nighthawk's mount, while others moved through the herd, urging the cattle into motion. Twenty minutes later they were gone, running west towards Albuquerque and the Rio Grande.

Back in Quemadero, in the early hours, Rufus suddenly opened his eyes. He'd only been half asleep, but something brought him fully awake. First, there was a scuffling sound from around the trash cans below his window, then, muffled thumps from somewhere further into the town. 'Goddamn hogs an' dogs,' he mumbled, and returned to a fitful slumber.

At five minutes to eight o'clock, Beth Longfield was busying herself with papers behind her desk. Her smile was genuine, and her curly hair looked good in the early light, but there was nervousness in her manner.

'Good morning. Dare I ask if you slept?' she asked Rufus tentatively.

Rufus thought for a moment. 'Yeah, up until I got disturbed. You'd think at that time o' night, each an' every one of us would have homes to go to.'

'They're sayin' it was the Rosado,' Beth said.

'O' Lordy, not the *Rosado*,' Rufus kindly mocked. 'Has it been said, what they were up to?'

'Yes.' Beth wasn't going along with Rufus's attitude. 'They broke into the bank, took boxes of ammunition from the hardware store, and stole a herd from the Ancho Arena. They took in the Buchanan Bank as well.'

'They're sure gettin' around,' Rufus said, almost respectfully. 'Not bad for a wagon load o' cats. I wonder what Emile Rednapp makes of it all.'

'Why don't we take a ride out there and ask him?' It was Eady. She was still buckling on her gunbelt as she came into the room. '*Now* would be a good time to avail ourselves of his offer o' work.'

'Hello. I don't think so,' Beth greeted Eady. 'Mr Rednapp's not exactly welcoming visitors.'

'That'll be since he last came to town,' Eady said. 'But Rufus is right. An' the man knows I'm not his enemy.'

'I hope you're right,' Beth said, and gave the sort of smile that Rufus liked.

'Yeah, well us two's goin' further down the street to take a bite. Let's *all* hope we'll be seein' you later,' Eady said amiably.

As Rufus and Eady left the Longfield, they paid no attention to the man wearing a bleached duster, who stood back on the boardwalk.

Nathan Greensleeves watched the pair until they turned into an small adobe canteen for their late breakfast. After a moment or two, he went for his horse and swung lazily into the saddle. Thinking about the demands that had been made upon him earlier, he rode slowly from the town. There was some planning to do, and he had to be real careful.

When they'd finished their working breakfast, Rufus and Eady ordered up two wraps of bread, cold eggs and cheese. Then they headed for the livery stable, where Pentland Betts was sitting out front, working hard on a fresh chaw.

'You headin' to or from trouble?' he asked, spitting juice at the same time.

'Probably both,' Rufus answered him. 'So we need to hire fresh horses.'

'Leave the roan, else take your pick,' Betts said.

They looked over the stock that were stalled alongside their own bayo and sabino mounts.

'Nothin' more'n a couple o' cold-blood duns,' Rufus said.

'Well, that's all we want,' Eady replied.

Ten minutes later they were saddled up and leaving the livery.

'How'd we get to the Ancho Arena?' Rufus asked.

'Turn west. Five miles out, there's a bend in the river. If you're still livin', you'll see a sign tellin' you you're there,' Betts said, spat more dark stuff into the ground between his boots.

'So, what is it you know that we don't?' Eady asked him.

The livery man had another lengthy and fearsome dribble, before answering. 'I know about Emile Rednapp. An' after last night, he'll be givin' orders to shoot people.'

9

THE HENCHMAN

As Rufus and Eady rode into the street, Barton Frimley was swinging his own horse away from the hitching rail out front of the Tall Top saloon. The owner of the Barley Parcel was headed towards the western end of the town and the wagon road beyond.

'Somethin's burnin',' Rufus said. 'I hope it don't turn out to be us.'

'Why should it be?' Eady replied, as they too, were looking that way. 'Unless he's been talkin' to Betts, he don't know where we're goin'.'

'Yeah, I never thought o' that,' Rufus called out as he went ahead.

When they'd nearly ridden the five miles, Rufus glanced back. There was no one trailing them, and the town looked as peaceable as it had when they'd first ridden in.

'I reckon now's when you take a diversion, Eady.

Stay to the north, an' keep me in sight. If you hang in close to the water, there's old timber an' vine stuff to cover you. If there is anyone out there, you'll see 'em when they make their move on me. Just make sure you hit 'em, you hear? We're almost tippin' onto Rednapp's land.'

'Stop worryin', Rufe,' Eady said. She wheeled her horse and, spectacularly low in the saddle, kicked dust in a long, sweeping curve.

Ten minutes on, when the drygulcher fired, Rufus drew his feet from the stirrups, slid out of the saddle and hit the ground hard. He rolled over, kept going until he reached the shelter of a big, gnarled juniper at the side of the dirt road. 'I meant hit 'em before they hit me,' he yelled, spluttering dust.

A second bullet gouged out grit and stones from near Rufus's head. 'Goddamn Sharps Big Fifty,' he growled, at the sound of the gunshot. Gives the son-of-a-bitch some advantage, he mused wryly, his fingernails clawing at tree bark. Then, thinking of the rifle's lead power, he coiled himself snake-like.

The gun roared again, and its sound cracked like a thunderbolt. No bullet arrived though, and Rufus sensed the .50-calibre shot went straight to the cloud-less sky.

'Eady! You got him?' he shouted, and grinned hopefully. He waited, then got to his knees, held his hat against the brightness. He couldn't see the dun, but no more shots came and he wondered about calling again for Eady's attention. He didn't, just in case the rifleman was waiting to nail him proper.

But then, he heard her. 'You comin' in, Rufe? I got me some kind o' catfish down here,' she called.

Rufus crouched, made his way forward. Ahead and to his left, was the tangle of waterside vegetation, where the rifleman had been hiding out.

But now Eady was standing there, deep in sedge. With her boot, she'd been pressing the long barrel of a hefty rifle hard across Nathan Greensleeves' throat. 'Recognize anythin' down here?' she asked, as Rufe moved in.

Rufus grabbed at the front of the man's shirt and pulled him to his knees. 'Could have seen him in town,' he said uncertainly. Then he had a closer look at the garter the man wore around his wrist. 'This'll be a Rosado trinket, accordin' to Wheat Cater. But I ain't so certain, Eady. It's all a bit too pat. He is goin' to wake up, isn't he?'

'Yeah, I never got to shoot him.'

They both heard the clatter and splash of hoofs through loose stone. Looking quickly towards the sound, Rufus pulled up the big rifle, and Eady turned her Colt. Two riders were standing their horses across the shallow bed of the river. Eady relaxed, but not quite enough to lower her gun when she recognized the man.

'Must have been peaceable out here once,' Rufus remarked, as the riders walked on through the gently flowing water.

'What's goin' on here?' young Max Rednapp called out.

'This turkey woulda drygulched me,' Rufus

answered. 'Thought at first it was one o' your men.'

'He's a goddamn Rosado,' Rednapp blurted.

'I'm not so sure, kid. I reckon we're supposed to think that,' Rufus said. But his interest was on the girl who was riding the mare with 8 burned into its rump – the O Twist brand.

Rednapp saw the look. 'Seen somethin' you like, mister?' he challenged.

'I'm sorry,' Rufus smiled. 'Don't mean no disrespect.'

'This is Polly Hench. Her pa owns the horse ranch,' Rednapp said. 'Polly, meet Eady Dix an' Rufus Breese.'

Both Rufus and Eady nodded. Rufus tipped his hat. He let the Sharps' barrel drop back down, as Greensleeves started to move.

Eady saw the Hunch girl looking at her, a searching, dubious gaze, from the man lying at her feet up to the irregular outfit and muddy smudge across her chin. 'This is someone who don't go too fancy on introductions,' she said, over the curses and groans.

'Name's Greensleeves . . . work for Frimley. Got drygulched . . . not how they'll be telling it,' Greensleeves lied.

Rufus shook his head disbelievingly and turned to Rednapp. 'This don't say much for who's signed on to Frimley's payroll, does it?'

'Yeah. I mean, *no*. You're right. My pa's goin' to enjoy tenderizing this piece o' meat.'

'Mine too,' Polly Hench added.

Greensleeves seethed air from his bruised throat.

He shivered as cold sweat broke across his shoulders, wondered how much time he'd got left as a hired gun.

'Shut up,' Rufus snarled, as he dragged the man to his feet.

As Eady took a step back, a voice resonated from behind a deeply scarred juniper. 'Any o' you buckos makes a move, an' the pretty girl gets to lose her face.'

A man with a print shirt that was turned loosely around his head, moved aside thick streamers of vine. He was holding a shotgun that was aimed unswervingly at Polly Hench.

10

SAWBUCKS

'Get yourself moving, Nate. Forget that cannon an'
go for your horse. You'll live,' the man shouted.
Then he seemed to drift away, blend into the dense
growth that close-bordered the Rio Gargara.

Greensleeves had suddenly got hold of another
day. He pushed at Rufus, but he was still wary,
nervous as he stalked towards the bend in the river.

But Max Rednapp was less so. He dug his spurs,
knowing that if the masked man did fire, he'd collect
most of the shot. In an instant, Max and his pure-
bred chestnut were shielding Polly Hench from the
threatened blast.

'Goddamnit it, I thought it was me about to get
peppered,' Eady said.

'Must be them duds, Eady. Sort o' takes the
emphasis away from your face,' Rufus wavered. 'Now
let's go!' he shouted. 'No one's gettin' far.'

They headed upstream, Eady to the left, and Rufus to the right. But, surrounded by the highlights and shadows of dense timber, the man had vanished.

Eady stood silent, peered intently into the green tangled growth. Rufus went a little further, before backtracking.

'He's gone,' he said, angrily. 'I thought it was only Injuns could do that. Makes you think, don't it? Maybe they were both renegades . . . Rosados.'

'Yeah, maybe,' Eady agreed, not entirely convinced. 'I'm thinkin' more o' the one with the shotgun. I've heard the voice before . . . just can't tag it,' she said more seriously. Then, 'Rufe, look out there.'

Rufus shifted his attention to where Eady was pointing at a rider in the near distance. 'Greensleeves . . . an' on his own,' he said. Then he asked if it was Barton Frimley's voice that she'd recognized.

'No, wasn't him. But he's sure got some explainin' to do,' Eady promised.

'Yeah, an' meantime we still got company,' Eady said.

They returned to where Max and Polly sat their saddles waiting. It wasn't that Max lacked nerve for a chase, more that someone had to look out for Lyman Hench's daughter. Even so, they decided it was foolhardy, an unnecessary risk to search any further for the man with the shotgun.

It took them nearly fifteen minutes to retrieve the dun mounts, and when they all rode from the river,

Max and Polly were out front. They were nearing the Pecos wagon road, when another group of horsemen appeared from the direction of Quemadero. It was Yule Arnold, and he was flanked by Emile Rednapp and Stub Jessel, Rednapp's ever present foreman.

'Can't be anyone left in town. *Now's* a good time to rob it blind,' Rufus muttered.

Eady nodded eagerly. 'If we weren't havin' such a fine of time out here,' she said, with a giggle.

'What's been happenin'?' Arnold enquired. 'We been out to some o' the smaller ranches . . . hearin' their troubles. We heard the sound of a big gun.'

'This is gettin' real tiresome, Sheriff. Why'd should it be *us* who knows what's goin' on? I'm beginnin' to think we should take to the hills. An' that probably goes for Eady, too.'

Arnold took a deep, steadying breath, looked quickly at Eady who was nodding.

'An' what's my boy doin' with the Hench kid?' Emile Rednapp, growled.

'Only me an' Polly know that. Why not ask *us*?' Max spoke up defiantly.

'Have you got something against me, Mr Rednapp?' Polly asked, a touch chilly. 'I thought we were all on friendly terms.'

Rednapp's nostrils flared above his flowing white moustache. 'I don't have to explain to you,' he said.

'Ease up, Emile,' the sheriff advised. 'They ain't your beeves to push around.'

'Well, as of late, I ain't got too many o' *them* left,' the rancher responded sourly.

'An' that's why you don't want to go upsettin' your neighbours,' Arnold reasoned. 'Some of 'em are in the same boat, an' gettin' a mite proddy.'

'Goddamnit it, maybe I got good reason to go upsettin' one or two of 'em. You thought o' that yet, Sheriff?' The implication was clear in Rednapp's hardening tone.

'That's a slur on my pa. Just wait till he hears,' Polly said. She wheeled her mare away, and Emile Rednapp's eyes narrowed.

'Caution don't mean much to you, does it, Pa?' Max said, disappointedly.

Stub Jessel moved his horse forward a step. 'Let her go, boss. No harm done in lettin' 'em know what you're thinkin',' he said.

'He acts more like a bell mule than a foreman,' the sheriff observed, with some obvious concern.

Jessel glared at Arnold, moved his right hand closer to his gun.

The sheriff puckered his lips and sucked air noisily. 'My best years might have gone, Jessel, but I can still put the likes o' you in the ground,' he snarled threateningly.

'He means it, Stubb,' Rednapp barked at his man. 'Back off.'

Rufus winked at Eady. 'It's goin' to be hard to leave here,' he said. 'These folk exude such a sense o' neighbourliness.'

'Well let's stay for a while, find out what Rednapp's goin' to do,' Eady suggested.

'I pity who meets up with *them* next,' Arnold

muttered as they sat watching Emile Rednapp ride off, with his son a couple of lengths behind. 'Tell me about you gettin' shot at,' he said.

'Someone tried to drygulch us . . . well, *Rufus*. We'd been figurin' on somethin' o' the kind, so I was set on puttin' a stop to it. Then young Rednapp showed up with Polly Hench.' Eady attempted a convincing smile for the sheriff. 'The one out for sneak shootin' was called Greensleeves . . . Nate Greensleeves. Unfortunately he ain't with us any more.'

'You shot him?'

'No, we never fired a round. He's a lucky sumbitch . . . had some kind o' sentinel turn up. They both clean-heeled it.'

Arnold considered Eady's brief story, but wasn't entirely satisfied. 'This pair are appointed deputies,' he explained, changing tack. 'They rode from Tucumcari, lookin' for information on the Rosado.'

Eady and Rufus nodded at the two men. 'You know o' this Nate Greensleeves?' Eady asked them. Both deputies shook their heads.

'We're headed back to town,' Arnold said. 'I forgot to lock it. You ridin' with us?' he asked.

Rufus was looking at Eady and grinning. 'Reckon we're stayin' here,' he said. 'Any minute now, we're expectin' Beth Longfield to arrive with cakes an' a band. We'll probably be back at nightfall.'

Eady watched the deputies riding towards Quemadero with the sheriff. 'Them's a pair to chew the dog with,' she said. 'They never said a word.'

'Yeah, two o' the wise monkeys. Sheriff didn't seem too troubled about not goin' back to town with him,' Rufus said, thoughtfully.

'Should he be?' Eady wondered.

'Seein' as we're beatin' most o' the trouble from cover, you'd think he'd want to keep a lawful eye on us.'

They rode nearly two miles from the wagon road, dismounted under the shade of an old live-oak and ground hitched the horses. Rufus unfastened his saddle-bag for the cold food, but drew out a small, flat packet.

'Strange; how'd this get here?' he said, unfolding the packet and staring at a wad of crisp bills.

'Are they what I think . . . sawbucks?' Eady wanted to know.

'Yeah, about fifty of 'em.' Rufus mumbled incredulously. 'There's somethin' written, says:

> *Boss, we're ready for Quemadero and Buchanaro.*
> *Rosados are riding east and west*
> *Nate.*

Rufus studied the words for a few seconds, then he gave a big laugh. 'Jeez, Eady, what sort o' joker set this up?' he said.

Eady wasn't quite so diverted. 'If the sheriff found all that under your saddle, you'd be nominated chief o' these tiresome Rosados,' she pointed out. 'You've been hornswoggled, Rufe, an' that means me, too.'

Rufus riffled the bills. 'Except o' course, we ain't,'

he grinned. 'Besides, as soon as they pulled the next job, we'd be as free as meadow larks. Oh, an' we just been funded.'

11

THE PRIME SUSPECTS

Rufus and Eady sat beneath the weather-beaten oak. Rufus held on to the folding money and Eady looked at the note.

'What you thinkin' of?' Rufus asked.

'I'm thinkin' there's a tang of doubt about Ida Rose an' her Rosados. I'm thinkin' maybe we shouldn't joke about ridin' on.'

'How'd you mean?'

'Why'd they keep up that kind of activity? You can only take so much revenge . . . settle so many scores. I'm thinkin' what if it's someone takin' advantage of the legend o' them soiled sisters. Hah, it wouldn't be the first time.'

Rufus levelled a straight look at Eady. 'You think the guilt's elsewhere?' he asked with developing interest.

'Yeah. Well, not bein' quite as they seem. Call it a gut feelin'.'

'Huh, well in that case I ain't standin' around with five hundred dollars in my mitt.'

Rufus took a close look at the gnarled bark that twisted and curled its way around the old tree. He selected a deep vertical cleft in the timber, and wedged the fold of money in deep. Then he peeled and pressed in bleached shards to seal the cache.

'This old character's done its growin'. Let's hope a wanderin' peckwood don't decide to make its home here,' he said, disappointed at the outcome.

With a final look around, Rufus and Eady collected their horses and rode back to the wagon road.

Yule Arnold was hunkered in the shade of his big-bellied horse, quietly waiting.

'I was right,' Rufus sighed, as they got near. 'He's come to take us in. You best shoot him, Eady.'

The sheriff interpreted the situation. 'You just keep away from them firearms. Particularly you, lady,' he said agreeably. 'I got lucky findin' you. But there ain't too many places out here where you can hide.'

'What is it you're wantin' then, Sheriff?' Eady asked him.

'Ogden Rimsayle wants to set up a meetin'. I forgot to say, earlier.'

'Must've been important to risk sun-stroke, Sheriff?' Rufus said drily.

Arnold smiled at the fair and obvious response. 'Don't remember him givin' me any detail. But he's a bank manager, so I'm sure you'll find it *is*,' he said.

On the ride back to Quemadero, the sheriff answered questions about the local ranches, what he thought on the return of the Rosados. 'This could be the start o' big trouble across the territory,' he admitted. 'Last night's got me most worried.'

'Any murder shoulda done that,' Rufus remarked, coldly.

'Do you believe this Ida Rose has come back from the dead?' Eady asked.

'Not from the dead, no,' he said and smiled. 'I never did think she was behind what these so-called Rosados are doin'.'

'Why not?' Eady pressed.

'Rose had somethin' to her. It's hard to put into words. She had her own mind . . . would have taken that wrong an' made good of it . . . seen it as a second chance.'

As they rode into the western end of town, Eady again felt the twinge of unease. If Arnold was right, she wondered, who had been putting up Ida Rose as a resurrected thief and murderer? Eady had begun to suspect that it was someone's gainful decoy.

The three riders pulled up in front of the bank as Ogden Rimsayle came out to welcome them.

'Ah, you found them, Yule,' he said. 'I was fearing they might object.'

The two deputies stepped out from the bank. Ominously, they moved close behind the sheriff as he

72

dismounted. Rufus and Eady shared a quick glance, then they, too, climbed from their horses, dropped their reins across the hitching rail.

'We ain't done nothin' to object to,' Rufus answered back. 'The sheriff said you wanted to see us.'

No one spoke for a moment, and the teeth of the big doubt snapped at Eady. She looked at Rufus, saw the same thing had just happened to him. They were the prime suspects, and they had ridden in peaceably for their punishment.

'Sorry, but there weren't an alternative . . . not up against *your* guns,' Arnold admitted. 'Ogden here says he can prove you're with the Rosado . . . that you raided the bank in Buchanan.' Arnold saw the deep dawn of alarm on the faces of Eady and Rufus. 'An' there's a murder or two that I ain't forgettin',' he continued. 'But o' course, he's got to prove it.'

'He sure has, Sheriff,' Rufus said, his whole body tense. 'Me an Eady insist upon it.'

'Go on, search them,' Rimsayle practically ordered Arnold. 'I'm informed they're carrying money from the Buchanan Bank.'

'An' I'm tellin' you, we ain't got more'n twenty bucks between us,' Rufus bit out the words at Rimsayle.

'They'll be ten dollar bills, fresh from the Denver Mint. See for yourself, Yule,' Rimsayle demanded.

Before the sheriff could make a move, Barton Frimley and Wheat Cater walked from the Tall Top saloon. The two men looked to see what was happening, crossed the street to the bank. Rufus thrust a hand into a pants pocket, cursed silently as his fingers touched a piece of crumpled paper.

Rimsayle saw the anxious look that Rufus gave Eady. 'Search them,' he insisted impatiently.

'OK, take a look at their traps,' the sheriff indicated to the deputies.

The Tucumcari lawmen set to work searching the saddle-bags on the two hired duns. They found nothing, and Rimsayle had to suppress his raging frustration.

'What's cookin', Sheriff?' Cater asked, as he and Frimley got close. 'Don't look much like a social gatherin'.'

'Ogden's been informed that these two are Rosado chiefs, an' they're packin' bills to prove it,' Arnold said,with a clear pinch of amusement. 'For the *Examiner*'s editor, it almost seems a shame they ain't.'

'Who the hell's givin' *you* information like that, Rimsayle?' Cater sneered, his animosity towards the banker plain to see.

'Go through their clothes,' Rimsayle bellowed, with renewed indignation.

'I'm not here to—' Arnold started off. But he was immediately outdone by Rufus.

'The first man to touch me, dies. Lawman or not,' he threatened, his eyes now blazing with intent.

'You heard him, Sheriff,' Eady offered. 'None of you's come here to die. Rufus told you what we're carryin'. But I'll give you somethin'.' She pulled out

74

the garter she'd taken from Speke Dancer's body. She'd almost forgotten it was in her pocket.

'An' I got *this*,' Rufus said, holding up the note that was supposedly from Nathan Greensleeves.

'What you got there?' Cater asked.

The sheriff took the note and read out the few words.

Cater shook his head, stared at Eady and Rufus. 'Well, ain't you two a let down,' he said ruefully.

Frimley fingered the side of his face where Rufus had punched him. 'Can't say I'm too surprised,' he jeered. 'They ain't the sort to abide with any civilized laws.'

Rufus and Eady didn't respond. They knew that words were futile, making a fight of it would be fatal.

'Guess there's no need to tell you you're both under arrest,' Arnold said jadedly.

With Arnold and the deputies surrounding them, Rufus and Eady started off down the street to the jail. By not removing their guns, it was Arnold's way of making it less obvious that the two strangers to Quemadero were being taken into custody.

Rufus glanced back over his shoulder, back towards the bank. Cater, Rimsayle and Frimley remained out front, but he gleaned little from the look of them.

12

THE WAY OUT

Along the Tio Gargara, a hunting fox peered from the twisted roots of a seep-willow, barked his excitement at a snake that swam the slow-water. The sharp sound drifted to the cell window of Quemadero's jail.

'At least you're free,' Eady Dix, said dejectedly. She sat on the edge of a broken palet staring at Rufus. Until it got too dark, she'd been reading the adobe wall carvings of former occupants.

'Horell Totty? What sort o' name's that?' she asked. 'Wonder what they did wrong?'

'This is Quemadero, so probably not much,' Rufus answered, without paying too much attention.

A while later, one of the deputies lit an oil lamp that was hanging in the corridor. It did little more than emphasize the intimidating closeness of the cell bars.

Rufus knew they were in danger, that it wouldn't

take much for the townsfolk to organize themselves into a lynch mob. 'It'll be a lingerin' taste for some of 'em,' he reminded them both.

'Some never do learn,' Eady agreed. 'Perhaps if we pulled our shirts over our heads an' whooped, they'll all leave town. That's a lastin' impression, too.'

Rufus grinned. 'It would be if you did it,' he said. Then he looked serious. 'I should've buried that note in the tree with the money.'

'An' maybe I shoulda thought to mention it,' Eady muttered.

The confined pair were absorbed in their own thoughts, when the door along the corridor opened again. The same deputy appeared, but now, Wheat Cater was with him.

'Evenin',' Cater greeted, as he stepped up to the cell. 'Shame you ain't got separate quarters, but maybe it's more convenient. Can I have a private word with these two?' he then asked the deputy.

The man shrugged his shoulders, moved off, apparently unconcerned. Eady watched him go through the door, back to the sheriff's office. 'Only two reasons he'd do that,' she observed. 'He's either a real trustin' soul, or he's taken some boodle,' she responded to Rufus's questioning look.

'There's no reason why *I* shouldn't be trusted. It's a lot more'n can be said o' some. You know, the sheriffs gettin' more convinced about you an' the Rosado.'

'Is that meant to frighten us?' Rufus asked.

'Yeah, it sure is. You should be considerin' a quick

77

way out o' here.'

'The sheriff ain't *that* convinced. He won't let anythin' happen to us.'

Cater's forehead crinkled, his eyes squeezed a bit. 'Not if he could do somethin' about it,' he responded. 'But Rimsayle an' Clovis Finn are stirrin' the streets as we speak. There's a lot o' folk inclined to believe what they say.' The saloon keeper then pushed a Colt .45 through the bars. 'Take this,' he advised. 'Get out o' here, as soon as you can. If you don't you'll get your neck stretched . . . Eady too.'

Cater immediately stood off, as if to remove himself from what was happening. He turned and walked back to the office, his shadow wavering around the walls of the cell.

Rufus glanced at Eady, then sat down. They were both wearing their cartridge belts, but the sheriff had relieved them of their guns. Eady took the gun Cater had given Rufus, looked inquisitively at the chamber. She ejected the cartridges and replaced them with ones from her own belt. Then she placed the Colt beside her.

'Let's go after supper,' Rufus said. 'Right now, I'm hungry.'

Eady confirmed with a quietly controlled nod.

After they'd waited patiently for a long hour, the door at the end of the corridor opened. This time, it was Yule Arnold, and he was carrying a covered food platter.

'Longfield suppers are a way o' gettin' somethin' other than beans,' he said, good humouredly. 'Beth

78

said it's the end o' their fried chicken. Seemed to me, they was all eatin' somewhat plainer fixin's. You two must've touched a carin' spot. Still, it's an ill wind, an' there's coffee in the office.'

The sheriff held the tray in one hand, and unlocked the cell door with the other. Rufus and Eady stayed sitting calmly on their pallets, Eady using her hat to cover the gun.

'You been out dancin' with bank managers an' tinhorns?' Rufus ribbed unfunnily.

For a moment, Arnold looked uncertain. 'Eat the food,' he said, thinking on Rufus's words.

Ten minutes later, Eady wiped her mouth with the cloth that had covered the platter. 'The chicken was fine,' she said. 'I just hope it weren't our last supper.'

'There'll be no more lynch mobs in this town, if that's your meanin',' Arnold claimed from the cell doorway.

Rufus got to his feet and looked eagerly along the corridor. 'That's reassurin', Sheriff. I'll go get me some coffee on the strength of it,' he said intently.

'Yeah, me too,' Eady said, raising herself up.

Arnold took a faltering step back. 'What're you two doin'? Get on back in there,' he said.

Eady shook her head, drew the Colt from behind her back. She pushed the barrel gently against Arnold's fleshy jaw-line. 'You know better than to mistake this for a goddamn Rosado trick,' she advised with a chilly smile.

Rufus stepped forward and lifted the sheriff's Colt from its holster. He tried the balance and nodded his appreciation. 'I'll look after it for you,' he said.

'You're makin' an almighty big mistake,' Arnold said quietly.

Rufus removed the keys from where they were tucked into the sheriff's belt. 'We've been told recently, it would be an even bigger one to stay,' he said, and locked the cell door.

With Arnold sitting disconsolately, Rufus used a second key to unlock the narrow rear door of the jail. He dropped the keys to the ground, drew back the upper and lower bolts. Cool air swept in, and he looked out into the deep darkness. Clouds glowed yellow and grey in front of the moon, and there was the whiff of approaching rain.

'Careful, Rufe,' Eady whispered. 'I'm beginnin' not to like this.'

'I know, Eady, but we ain't goin' back,' Rufus said, as he moved off into the night.

13

THE ROAD TO
ANCHO ARENA

Eady was close behind Rufus when they cleared the
jail. They'd lost cover from the small building, when
a blast of gunfire exploded from the shadows. Rufus
felt as though a lump of skin was bitten from his left
arm, knew he'd just missed a more deadly bullet.

His mind's eye retained the after-image of the
flash, but in the dark, peripheral vision he saw a
moving figure. He fired off two shots. Eady was doing
the same, shooting at where the attacker was reck-
oned to be.

In the immediate silence that followed the
gunfire, they heard a painful, suppressed grunt, the
sound of a man falling hard to the ground. They
were hunkered down, their Colts covering open
ground ahead of them. In the darkness, a man lay

sprawled and lifeless, another took flight, his boots pounding the hard-packed dirt.

'Huh, I wager no one told 'em who we were,' Rufus rasped a few moments later. 'Must have been nearly a dozen, eh, Eady?'

'More like two, Rufe. Real leather-slappers would've had us easy.'

Eady reloaded her Colt, swung round as the rear door of the jail slammed open. Against the interior lamp, the shadowy profiles of two men loomed.

'Now, it's the deputies. We got to get out o' town,' Rufus advised quickly.

The pair ran from one dark blocky shape to another. Fifty yards in and out of the yards and outbuildings that backed the main street, a wedge of pale light fell through a half-open gate at the rear of the livery stable.

Rufus went through first, the palm of his hand in contact with the butt of his holstered Colt. He took cautious steps, squinted at the lantern that was hanging from a cross beam.

Pentland Betts stepped from the near end of the stalls. 'Should've guessed it would be you two,' he said, his walnut-stocked shotgun pitching between Rufus and Eady. 'No one else generates so many bullets. An' I told you about Rednapp's bad humour.'

'Yeah, you did,' Rufus agreed. 'Shame you could-n't have done likewise for those out back o' the poky. But I guess that was somethin' you couldn't have known about,' he added, as a restrained accusation.

Betts nodded as if he was thinking about it, moved

the twin barrels off target. 'Goddamn right,' he rasped. 'You owe me four dollars for the hire of them duns. The deputy brought 'em in.'

Eady was tense, alert for more trouble. Without taking her eyes off Betts, she reached into a pocket. She drew out a few bills, handed four over to the stable owner.

Betts lowered his shotgun, leaned it against the wall. 'Got to agree that jail don't provide much of a stopover,' he said. 'I was there once, for bein' drunk an' disorderly. Sheriff charged me in the mornin' for settin' fire to the goddamn cot.'

'Why'd you do it?' Eady asked.

'I didn't. It was burnin' long before I got into it.'

As the nervous laughter faded, Rufus and Eady heard the distinctive click of a gun's hammer being cocked.

But Eady had already turned to face the door, her right hand dragging at her Colt. She flinched to one side as she fired, the sound of her gun and that of the assailant merging as one booming blast. A bullet whistled by her head, thudded into the beam above the oil lamp.

Rufus swore, waved Betts away from the line of fire. Eady made another, more exacting shot through the doorway, held her aim and looked to Rufus, then Betts, who was reaching for his shotgun.

A man wearing a bleached duster staggered through the door. He took one pace forward, stopped, then took another.

'Greensleeves!' Rufus exclaimed. 'I'd've thought

Frimley would have you walkin' the Pecos by now . . . for derelictin' your duty.'

Eady stood very still. Breathing deeply she watched the man whom she had got the better of earlier. Her gun felt heavy, and she let it fall into her holster. She was suddenly worn down when she saw that the man called Greensleeves, was dying.

Greensleeves was slurring out curses as he took a last step forward. He slumped into a pile of fat grain sacks, groaned, and twisted his head to one side.

Rufus noticed the man was still wearing the garter around his wrist. 'Why'd you come back?' he asked.

'Had to,' he grated. 'I was only given a day or so.'

'What do you mean? Who you talkin' about?' Rufus demanded to know. He bent low over Greensleeves' body. 'Is this Rosado stuff?'

'Yeah. An' the boss weren't makin' a request.'

'The boss?' Rufus queried. 'Barton Frimley's your boss. What the hell's *he* got to do with the Rosado, or Ida Rose? Talk to me, feller. It might just save you, 'cause this time there's no one else,' Rufus said harshly.

'It ain't him . . . Frimley,' Greensleeves' voice was hardly audible. 'The one you're talkin' about's. . . .' But the man didn't say any more. His eyes opened, flickered and closed, then he rolled sideways on to the floor. 'You win this part,' he garbled, and his revolver fell from his dead fingers.

Betts stepped across the floor of the livery to pick up his shotgun. 'Never should've put this down,' he said, his eyes shifting uneasily from Rufus to Eady.

'What did you mean by savin' him . . . Greensleeves?' Eady asked Rufus.

'Nothin'.' Rufus said, and moved quickly to collect his gear. The two of them saddled their own sabino and the bayo mares, while Betts stood guarding the back door.

'Keep a hold o' that shotgun,' Rufus advised him, as they readied to leave. 'Next person through that door ain't goin' to be no merry-andrew.'

'Reckon I'll be OK,' Betts muttered enigmatically, as Rufus and Eady spurred their mounts into the darkness.

14

THE VISITORS

They were nearly two miles outside of Quemadero, when Eady pulled up beside Rufus.

'Are we headed where I think we're headed, Rufe?' she asked him.

'Yeah, the place we been meanin' to get to.'

'Well, let's rest up a minute. We can put somethin' around that wound while the light's with us.'

'It ain't more'n a bite . . . don't hurt none, Eady. It's best we ride,' Rufus answered, and spurred his sabino back into a lope.

A few miles beyond where they'd run into Nathan Greensleeves' Big Fifty rifle, the sign for the Ancho Arena ranch was strung between the boughs of two live-oak trees. There was a concentration of timber that clumped along the Rio Gargara. It was dark and forbidding, and Rufus shivered with apprehension.

He walked the mare forward, his sweaty hand gripping the butt of his Colt.

As together they pulled their mounts through the green shadows of the willow and mesquite, two armed men stepped out to confront them.

'Where're you two goin'?' one of them demanded.

'I reckon we're already there,' Rufus replied, smartly. 'We come to see Emile Rednapp.'

The lookout threw an interested glance towards Eady. 'What's your business?' he growled.

'That's for him to know.'

'He ain't seein' visitors,' the man continued aggressively.

'He'll see us,' Eady said.

Eady and her response surprised the man. 'Get the horses, Mano,' he said. 'They don't look like they're here to cause trouble.'

Mano stepped back into the trees, reappeared almost immediately leading two horses by the reins. The lookouts pushed their rifles into the saddle boots and mounted, indicated for Rufus and Eady to ride ahead.

For another three miles, the four rode in silence. Then the lights from a sprawl of buildings flickered through the night.

'Jeez. We must've reached Amarillo,' Rufus said in surprise.

They rode forward to one of two hitching rails that flanked the front terrace of the immense ranch house. The lookout who'd first challenged them swung from his horse and looped his reins.

Rufus and Eady reined in their own mares, while the other man sat his saddle and watched anxiously.

'Wait here,' Mano said. 'Who is it wants to see Mr Rednapp?'

'Rufus Breese an' Miss Eady Dix,' Rufus told him.

Mano cast another sceptical eye at Eady. 'Don't see too many o' your sort in these parts,' he muttered. Then he shrugged and took the terrace steps.

Rufus was growing restless, Eady even more so when Mano came back, two minutes later.

'Herm,' he called to his partner. 'It's OK to bring 'em in.'

The man named Herm dismounted, followed Rufus and Eady up the broad steps. First dark was almost on them and the first rain splattered against the deep overhang.

They went through the front door into a high-vaulted hallway. There were many doors off, and Navaho rugs lay across the scrubbed, puncheoned floor. Mano stopped and knocked at the door directly in front of them.

They heard Rednapp's voice, then Mano opened the door and motioned them into a step-down room with big furniture. Among the trappings of a rich and successful cattleman, Emile Rednapp sat in a thickly upholstered wing-back. He was holding a glass of amber liquid, looking up at them confidently.

'Good evenin',' he said. 'Mano tells me you've got vital business. It must be, to risk both your lives.'

'It's all to do with *worth*, Mr Rednapp,' Rufus said. 'So, we reckon it was them riskin' *theirs.*'

'Confidence and foolishness are occasional bed-fellows,' Rednapp acknowledged Rufus's bravado. 'All right, boys, you can get back to work now,' he told Mano and Herm.

Rednapp waited a moment for the men to close the door behind them. 'So, what is it brings you here?' he asked.

Rufus got the nod from Eady to tell him. 'Not so long ago, we were arrested, accused o' bein' leadin' lights o' the Rosado gang,' he said calmly. 'We just got through with escapin' from jail.'

'Well, I don't rightly know what to make o' that,' Rednapp said, looking from Rufus to Eady. 'It sounds very much like *your* vital business, not mine.'

'I think it *is*, Mr Rednapp. It was *your* cattle the Rosados stole, after raidin' the Buchanan an' Quemadero banks.'

'So?' Rednapp pressed.

'So, while Eady here was readin' inmates' histories, I got to wonderin' what you're doin' about it. You helped string Ida Rose from the branch of an old oak. Now, you're surroundin' yourself with armed guards, 'cause you think she's sprung from her grave.'

Rednapp shook his head. 'I never helped. Nor did Max. We were witnesses.'

Rufus grunted. 'Makes no odds,' he said. 'Tell us why you an' the rest of the ranchers around here just don't head 'em up an' move 'em out. Whoever they are, they're murderers an' stock thieves.'

'How do you know we ain't? An' what makes you two so interested?' Rednapp asked.

Eady's eyes narrowed. 'That's a dumb question . . . considerin'. I'll tell him,' she said.

Eady then told about what had happened to her and Rufus since the previous morning. How they'd found the body of Speke Dancer at Longfields, about the door being pushed to, and the attempt of Nathan Greensleeves to shoot them down. She spoke of the money, and the note that Rufus had discovered in his saddle-bags.

Rufus explained how Wheat Cater had given them a gun to help them escape from the jail. Of the men who'd tried to shoot them down as they did so. Then, Greensleeves' doomed attempt to kill them in the livery stable. 'An' *that's* what makes us interested, Mr Rednapp,' Rufus concluded.

'Put like that, it sure sounds like someone's mighty anxious to get your blood spilled,' Rednapp conceded. 'It's beginnin' to look like there's more than a wronged crib girl gettin' revenge.'

'Yeah, them's my feelin's too,' Eady said. 'There's got to be an explanation where money or such-like's involved. For instance, I heard someone say the railroad's layin' down a spur from Albuquerque.'

'Maybe these Rosado dames heard it, too,' Rufus contributed. 'Want to start brandin' ahead o' the roundup.'

'Yeah, that's a notion,' Rednapp said. 'With Speke already dead, that leaves three big ranches between the rivers. Lyman Hench, Barton Frimley an' me. If we were to follow old Speke, there'd be someone buyin' at bottom dollar. Max is my only kin, the same with Hench an' his daughter. Frimley's got none that are close.'

Eady nodded. 'Could be why he sees us as trouble. We got to get ourselves a plan for stayin' alive, Mr Rednapp. Let's say, that's what you owe.'

'Yeah, I remember. Anythin' else on your mind?'

'A couple o' things. Why's a man as powerful as you, buildin' a reputation for bein' pushed around?'

Rednapp ran the knuckles of his left hand across his moustache. 'Got anyone particular in mind?'

'Wheat Cater, for one. I'm interested 'cause maybe it matters.'

'An' maybe it don't. Maybe it'll be for me to know, an' for me to deal with, if that *is* what he's doin'.'

'Fair enough,' Eady accepted doubtfully.

Rednapp clicked the base of his glass on a table that had carved buffalo heads at each of its four corners. 'You said a couple o' things?' he reminded Eady.

Eady tried a smile. 'You were givin' your kid an' the Hench girl a hard time. I wondered why.'

Rednapp's blood colour rose. 'That's borderin' on insolence, Miss Dix. Be careful,' he warned.

'Hell, you must have been young once,' Eady countered. 'I'm just sayin' it's like a lot o' things round here . . . mighty unreasonable. Maybe that matters too.'

'The trouble's between me an' Lyman Hench. It don't matter to you. Now it's late, so I'll be thankin' you to—'

Rednapp was mid-sentence when a rear window shattered with a crash. The bullet thumped past Rufus and embedded itself in the timber-panelled wall.

Rednapp swore, immediately blew out the reading lantern beside him. Eady doused a wall sconce and Rufus did the same for the hanging lamp. The vast room was plunged into darkness as the tall, centre front window exploded.

'How many more goddamn bullets are goin' to miss?' Rufus said, his voice abrasive. 'An' we know it ain't Greensleeves.'

'Ida Rose has arrived. I been wonderin' how long,' Rednapp muttered.

'It sounds like they've got us in a fair grip, whoever it is,' Rufus responded. He held the layout of the room, in the deep dark, made it to the nearest window. He couldn't see much in the weak light from the ranch's outbuildings, but a volley of gunfire suggested the bunkhouse was also being hit.

'How many men you got out there?' Eady asked.

'At this time, maybe a dozen,' Rednapp said. 'Some of 'em will have gone into town.'

'If this *is* Ida Rose, why's she come right in here?' Rufus asked. His voice now had a severe edge, was uncompromising.

'Yeah, what the hell's goin' on?' Eady said, kicking

shards of glass across the floor.

The ranch owner was now standing alongside the other wrecked window. 'I was more than a witness: I helped string her up,' Rednapp confessed in the rousing atmosphere.

15

THE SANCTUARY RAID

'You thinkin' what *I'm* thinkin'?' Rufus called out as more gunshot peppered the house.

'Similar lines, maybe,' Eady answered. 'That we're in real trouble.'

'A rifled cannon couldn't put shot through these timbers.' Rednapp railed.

'That's true. But if it is Ida Rose, she'll burn the place down. An' from what you say, who's to blame her?' Rufus countered.

'Why the hell didn't your two lookouts do somethin' about it?' Eady added to the rebukes. 'They coulda fired a warnin' shot.'

'They rode south-west. This murderous bunch would have come in from Conchas Lake. That's *north-west* o' here.'

'How do we know it ain't Yule Arnold and his two chatty deputies?' Rufus asked, as he edged to the corner window.

'They wouldn't be shootin' up the place, for God's sake,' Rednapp snapped.

'Yeah. I reckon Rose's desire to gut Mr Rednapp, is more'n Arnold wantin' us back in his rotten jail,' Eady said.

Rufus grunted, pushed his Colt through the shattered window beside Rednapp and loosed off two shots into the darkness.

'What guns do you keep here?' Eady asked Rednapp.

'Enough to ward off any goddamn Rosados. There's six rifles on the rack, an' I got two army revolvers in the drawer.'

'Good. We'll need 'em if it's the last stand,' Eady said. She was still peering from the side of the window, when she glimpsed someone in a gleaming wet slicker. She took a fast shot and swore. 'Your boys in the bunkhouse can slow 'em down a bit,' she suggested, 'keep 'em from comin' through the front door.'

The rain had eased and the sky had lightened, and Rufus moved a shutter across the open window. He watched, blinked, stared for another moment, until he was sure. Against the blue-black skyline he saw riders advancing from the far side of the home ground.

'Riders comin',' he said. 'If they're support for this bunch, we really ought to start diggin' a fraidy hole,' he said grimly.

Across the ranch-house yard, the gunfire suddenly grew more intense. 'Come an' see this, Eady,' Rufus called out. 'These fellers have got 'emselves their own little war.'

Rednapp stood back, and Eady took a slanting look out front of the house.

'Mine enemy's enemy . . . God bless 'em,' she murmured.

'You got a fittin' turn o' phrase on you, lady,' Rednapp said.

For a few minutes it sounded like the fighting stormed around the outbuildings, and on all sides of the house.

'Georgie Custer must've felt like this, atop o' that hill,' Rufus yelled.

'They killed him,' Rednapp pointed out. 'They killed *everyone*.'

The three of them faced into the room with their backs against the wall. They daren't move around or risk any more shooting from the windows for fear of hitting an ally.

Then abruptly, those who they thought were the Rosado gang, withdrew. They split up, ran for the deep shadows of the barns and sheds, then for the horses they'd tied in, back among the surrounding timber. The new arrivals were hard on their heels though, poured lead as their send off.

Eady could now see the handful of men who'd come to the aid of the Ancho Arena. 'Whoever they are, they look like they're friendly natives,' she said.

'Hey, Pa, you in there?' the strong, youthful voice of Max Rednapp hollered. 'We come to help you out some.'

'Who got with you?' Rednapp yelled back.

'Mister Hench. He's brought his men.'

'What's he expect for it?' Rednapp blustered.

'Try startin' with three or four fingers o' whiskey,' Rufus offered obligingly.

Max Rednapp had drawn in close to the front terrace. He was astride his thoroughbred chestnut, holding up a Winchester rifle. 'We got control. You can come out,' he confirmed.

From inside the house, a match flickered then glowed as Rednapp relit the table lamp. As the light spread, the three occupants looked around them. Glass was strewn across the floor and the wall panelling was splintered and holed from the attackers' bullets. There was a hole in and out of the wingback where Rednapp had been sitting less than ten minutes earlier.

'That would've given you more than a dose o' heartburn,' Rufus mused, as he and Eady sided Rednapp to the front of the house.

In the hallway they stopped. Rufus and Eady levelled their Colts, watched tensely as Max pushed the door open and inwards with the barrel of his rifle.

'You could've been in there with a gun to your head,' the young Rednapp said, with an uncertain smile. The men behind him stood hesitantly on the terrace steps.

97

'Come on in . . . all o' you. The drinks are on me,' his father said with some difficulty.

'Does that include me, Emile?' an ageing man with a deeply lined face, rasped.

'Yeah. I guess I owe you that, you ol' maverick.' Rednapp turned his big hawk nose at Lyman Hench.

Hench pulled his hat from his head and stepped forward stifly. 'Yeah, you do. Just don't expect me to light a peace pipe,' he grumbled.

Rednapp crossed the hallway with Hench, Max and one of the O Twist waddies. Eady and Rufus followed, held their ground when Stub Jessel suddenly appeared through a doorway beside the staircase. The Ancho Arena foreman was grimly eyeing the men who were going into Rednapp's living-room.

Eady and Rufus shared the same thought. Where was Jessel during the raid?

'You forgot to rub the sleep from your eyes,' Rufus said scornfully.

'Get off this ranch. You ain't wanted . . . either o' you,' Jessel snarled.

'You're pickin' a safe time to throw your weight around,' Rufus retaliated.

'Stub!' Emile Rednapp shouted from across the hallway. 'I give the orders under my own roof.'

'It's the reek o' the hoosegow, Mr Rednapp. It's stuck to 'em.'

'How the hell d'you know about that, Jessel? Unless you been stickin' an ear against one o' Mr Rednapp's doors,' Rufus fired off quickly.

'That ain't good, Stub.' Rednapp glared angrily at his foreman. 'You kissin' carpet, while we're bein' chopped up by Rosado bullets. Get back to the bunkhouse, an' pack your traps. I want you gone by mid-mornin' tomorrow.'

'Right. I'll go an' see if there's any town patrol work with Yule Arnold,' the foreman said. 'When the Tucumcari deputies go home, he'll be missin' someone to share confidences with,' was his tangible threat.

'Get out. We'll talk about it later,' Rednapp conceded.

'An' what about these two?'

Rednapp cracked his knuckles. 'Arnold might stump up some abettin' charge, if he finds out you're here . . . 'cause he's goin' to,' he said, his eyes flitting uneasily between Rufus and Eady. Rufus and Eady glared disappointedly at Rednapp, then defiantly at Jessel. Then they moved out on to the terrace, slowly took the steps to the yard.

'I don't understand it,' Eady said. 'Rednapp shouldn't be scarin' easy, but he *is*.'

'Yeah, Jessel's got somethin' on him. Somethin' that Rednapp wants kept from the sheriff. I wonder what it is?'

'Let's go back an' ask him?'

'No. We're headed straight back to Quemadero. We got to find some goddamn Rosado chiefs.' Rufus looked to the sky. The rain had drifted south, but the moon still glowed through the scudding clouds.

'What's on your mind, Eady?' Rufus asked, after

ten minutes of determined riding.

'I was thinkin' that young Max must have brought Hench and his best men tonight. But the Rosado would have got clean away, even with those waddies chasin' 'em.'

'Yeah; I'm not with you though,' Rufus said.

'Do you remember joshin' about the best time to rob Quemadero?'

Rufus nodded. 'Yeah, when everyone was out o' town.' He understood and grinned. 'So, on that reck-onin' Ida Rose should be runnin' straight for the O Twist?'

'Wouldn't *you*? But as long as Hench is back there sippin' Wild Turkey, I doubt it's dawnin' on him. You figure we should veer south a bit?'

'Hell no, Eady. I'd say we done our best by these big-shot ranchers,' Rufus decided.

Eady took off her hat, beat it a couple of times against her leg before replacing it. 'I knew you'd think that, Rufe,' she said. 'An' I seem to recall, the spread's about four miles off the wagon road. . . ?'

'Yeah, an' Polly Hench's features are more memo-rable than Yule Arnold's,' Rufus laughed into the night.

16

THE TRUTH OF IT

Eady flipped up the cover of a silver hunter, read the time by the flaring of a match.

'Where'd you get that ol' stemwinder?' Rufus asked.

'Coach company. Token o' gratitude for savin' those army provisions.'

'Is it workin'?'

'Yeah, says it's nearly exactly an hour off midnight,' Eady said, and tucked the watch back into an inner pocket.

They lapsed into a long silence as they rode. Each had their own thoughts on how they'd handle the situation ahead of them.

Eventually they topped a low rise, reined in among the heady fragrance of wild fleabane. Nestling at the bottom of the incline, they could make out the shadows of feed sheds, breaking pounds and stables.

'That'll be the Twist,' Eady said. 'Impressive, but it ain't lookin' too busy right now.'

'Hmm. It's meant to look like Sleepy Hollow,' Rufus said, after considering the layout. 'There ain't any lights, but there's someone down there. An' not just them who've got title.'

Across the hard-pummelled ground that fronted the ranch house, the front doorway yawned big and black in the shadows beneath the overhang. Eady and Rufus slid from their saddles, let the reins of their horses drop to the ground.

'That feelin' o' trouble's come back again,' Eady said quietly. 'I hope they don't have some big dog.'

They walked carefully up the steps, stopped to listen at a front window near to the open doorway. The window had a shade almost fully drawn, allowed a slice of yellow light to run across the sill. They just picked out the murmur of voices within, drew their Colts and edged their way through the doorway. From the left, they heard the voices again, though couldn't make out any words. Rufus pushed out his left hand and ran it along the wall, advanced towards where more light bled from under the closed door of the parlour.

Eady edged along until they both heard the voices more clearly. Barton Frimley of the Barley Parcel ranch was taking up the conversation.

'Young Rednapp ridin' in here had to be a ruse,' he said. 'A trick to get your pa out to the Arena.'

'Max wouldn't do that,' Polly Hench objected.

'You got to remember who he is, Miss Polly. But he

102

ain't strong enough to defy the old man.'

'But why would he do such a thing?' Polly persisted.

'It's the Rednapp way of endin' a grievance with your pa. I rode straight here, as soon as I heard.'

'Tell me what happened, Mr Frimley?' Polly said with rising anxiety.

'The Rosado were there waitin'. With a mix o' renegade Comanche, you couldn't tell 'em apart,' Frimley continued. 'None off 'em stood a chance. It looks like your pa knew too much, Polly. An' that's what it was all about.'

'I just don't believe you. What did he know too much about?' Polly said shakily. 'What *are* you doin' here?' The bleak, shock news started to weaken Polly's voice.

'Who do you think *were* the Rosados?' Frimley proposed unpleasantly.

Outside the room, Rufus's elbow jabbed at Eady. 'Hell. Do you reckon she's fallin' for this?' he asked.

'No,' Eady said, twisted the door handle and kicked. She stood threateningly in the opening, covered Frimley with her Colt. 'What nasty story are you feedin' this girl, you evil pig?' she asked icily.

Frimley was fifteen feet away, sitting opposite Polly Hench. 'You two . . . you're. . . .' He spat words in shock, grabbed at the arms of the chair.

'Don't get up. You'll go right back,' Eady threatened.

'Your pa's OK, Polly,' Rufus said. 'Max *did* take him an' some o' your men over to the Ancho Arena, an'

103

they drove off the Rosado gang. Right now they're gettin' roostered on the finest bourbon. We know, 'cause that's where we rode from.'

'O' course you did,' Frimley, butted in. 'I was in town when Arnold arrested you. He threw the pair o' you in jail, for bein' . . . with Ida Rose. When you broke out, you scrambled straight under Rednapp's wing.'

'An' that from a man who's just lied to you that your pa's dead,' Rufus said with open scorn.

Polly was shocked and bemused, looked from Eady to Rufus. 'You're sure he's not dead, Mr Breese?' she asked.

'Yeah, quite sure. Now, if you wouldn't mind turnin' away, me an' Mr Frimley need to get somethin' cleared up.'

With that, Rufus stepped forward and relieved Frimley of the revolver he carried beneath his coat. 'Can't have you thinkin' of makin' a fight back,' he said facetiously.

'What you goin' to do to me?' Frimley asked nervously.

Rufus knuckled the man hard and high in the side of his head. 'Jeeesus,' he snapped at the instant pain. 'How many *more* times am I goin' to have to do this?'

Eady swallowed hard and shook her head, thought back to what had happened in the dining-room of the Longfield.

'Now, you tell Miss Polly here, that you're a liar,' Rufus rasped impatiently at Frimley. 'Tell her that Max Rednapp is the fine young man she thinks he is.

Tell her, by Christ, or I'll find somethin' to crack your skull apart.'

'Your pa's OK,' Frimley groaned, 'As far as I know.'

'That's good,' Rufus told him. 'Saves us both any more hurt.'

Eady moved in and told Frimley to get up, nudged him towards the door. 'I'd think real serious about your next move,' she said.

'Ride off, an' ride far,' Rufus said, with genuine menace, when they were back in the doorway. 'If we ever meet up again, you'll be playin' gunnies with Miss Dix. Believe me, that ain't somethin' you want to look forward to.'

When Rufus and Eady went back into the house, they found that Polly had lighted some more lamps, around the house, another one in the parlour. She smiled with tearful relief as they came into the room.

'He's gone now?' she asked tiredly.

'Yeah, he's gone,' Rufus confirmed. 'Now, perhaps you can tell us what he was doin' here . . . what he *said* he was doin' here?'

Polly nodded. 'I heard him calling. I was in my room. I was just lying there . . . worried about Max an' Pa. He said Pa was badly wounded an' wanted to see me. He said he'd take me there.'

'Well, I guess he woulda done that,' Rufus sneered.

'He said, Max led Pa and our boys into a trap.'

'Yeah, we heard that bit. I wonder why he wanted to get you away from the ranch? There must've been some *other* reason,' Eady said, with a small, restrained smile.

'I know,' Polly nodded slowly. She was still puzzled, still worried.

'We got riders . . . again,' Rufus called out. 'If it's the Rosados, I'm goin' to shoot me some this time. Let's get ready.'

Cradling Frimley's revolver, Polly shut herself in the scullery at the rear of the house. Rufus and Eady remained in the parlour. They turned down the lamps and sat waiting in the darkness. In the ensuing silence, it wasn't long before Eady voiced her thoughts. 'Shootin' flies off army stores ain't exactly my idea o' pleasure, Rufe, but it's harmless compared to this,' she said quietly.

After a long five minutes, there was footsteps on the porch, then in the hall. When Lyman Hench appeared in the doorway, he was lighted by the weak light from the hallway lamp. Eady flicked another one of her matches and Rufus murmured an oath of relief.

Hench was momentarily surprised to be staring into the barrels of two Colts. But he wasn't a man to scare easy. 'What the hell you two doin' here?' he asked. 'Not that you ain't real welcome.'

'We'll get Polly, let her tell you,' Eady said. 'Me an' Rufus still got a meetin' planned with Sheriff Arnold.'

'Yeah, that's right,' Rufus agreed, and holstered his Colt. 'Now that some folk are acceptin' they ain't us, we ought to start doin' somethin' about these

Rosados.'

'Well, if that's what you want to do,' Hench said tiredly. 'I'm for hittin' the sack while I can still find it.'

17

THE WASTING

Rufus and Eady rode into Quemadero, into the near deserted back end of town. They stopped in front of the livery stable and Rufus dismounted. He handed the sabino's reins to Eady, went to the closed door of the stable and knocked. There was no answer, and he knocked louder. A full minute later, the door opened and Pentland Betts stood there fully dressed.

His jaw dropped and he groaned as he looked at Rufus, then beyond to Eady. 'This is a goddamn nightmare,' he muttered. 'Do you know what time this is?'

'Yeah, near enough. The horses don't, though. Can you take 'em in for the rest of the night?' Rufus asked. 'We're goin' back to the Longfield.'

'That's what you said an' did last time,' Betts said wryly.

'Yeah, on your recommendation,' Eady grinned,

as she climbed down from her bayo.

Betts stepped back inside, drew the bolts from the rest of the big door.

Rufus followed, noticed the body of Nathan Greensleeves had been removed. 'Incidentally, you were there, at Ida Rose's hangin', weren't you?' he said.

'Huh, I'll wager that nothin' you two does is *incidental*. But yeah, I might've been,' Betts answered, slow and foxy like.

'Who else?' Rufus's voice suddenly took on a harder edge.

'Wheat Cater, Speke Dancer an' July Tomkiss, the Rednapps an' Ben Longfield ... that's Beth's pa. There was seven, includin' me. I weren't for the lynchin' though, an' didn't stay. I never saw 'em string her up.'

'It certainly ain't *love* that's blind in this place,' Rufus said, as he led the horses in. His disgust at Betts trying to lessen his participation was clear.

Betts slammed the door shut after Rufus and Eady had walked from the stable. From just outside they heard the bolt sliding back into place.

'Hey, you remember Wheat Cater sayin' that not *all* your enemies are ever dead?'

'Yeah, I remember,' Rufus said. 'I wonder if he meant it personal?'

Warily, the two kept close to the town buildings' shadows. Halfway along the street, they turned into an alley that sided the Tall Top saloon.

'Let's hope he's at home,' Rufus said, nodding at

a door that had a window alongside it. He raised himself on his toes and looked in. 'Yeah, it's him; this is his office,' he murmured. 'Hey Cater,' he then called out. 'Let us in. We got to talk.'

Wheat Cater looked up quickly from his desk. His wide-awake eyes met Rufus's through the mire that smeared the window, and he made a move to unlock the door.

Inside the office, Eady locked the door and pulled down the window blind.

Cater turned back to his chair and sat down heavily. 'You two should be long gone,' he said, casting an eye on his Winchester above the door lintel.

'Yeah, it's still there,' Rufus said. 'But where'd you get the .45 you handed me in the cell?'

'Er, from right here. In this line o' business, you come by 'em now an' again. Does it matter?' Rufus and Eady exchanged a questioning glance. 'It mattered to Eady. She replaced the cartridges,' Rufus said.

Cater dragged out an aggrieved look. 'You thought I was settin' you up with some sort o' bluffer gun?'

'It could've been someone else. You didn't have to know about it,' Rufus countered more thoughtfully.

'Someone who'd do a thing like that? Well, I'd shoot 'em without ceremony. *You* ain't done it yet. So why not?' Cater insisted.

'You got yourself a good business here with the Tall Top?' Rufus asked.

'I got no debts.'

'Exactly. So why jeopardize that by runnin' around stealin' cattle, an' robbin' banks? An' you get to kill people lawfully from outside your own front door,' Rufus reasoned. 'No, it ain't you, Cater. You were never any boss, foot soldier, or even trail cook with the Rosado.'

The three were considering the state of affairs when there was a sharp rap on the alley door. They glanced at each other and Eady snapped up her Colt.

Cater went to the door, hesitated and looked back. 'Get in the store room until I find out what they want,' he whispered.

Rufus and Eady moved in with the saloon's consumables and pushed the door most of the way shut.

Cater unlocked and opened the door to the alley, stepped back when he was confronted by a tall, spare-framed figure who stood silently in the semi-darkness.

The woman's blue eyes bored deep into Cater's startled face. 'I been lookin' for you,' she said, her voice tough and steady. 'You were there, when we rode through the rain, when we stopped at the big live-oak. You were there, when they put the rope around my neck . . . heard me say I'd hunt you all like dogs.'

'Ida Rose,' Cater started. 'You don't look like . . . like you *did*,' he stuttered, the dread, cracking up his voice.

'I lost some pounds, an' I been nowhere near a saloon. You expect me to be wearin' satin an' lace, after bein' hanged an' shot an' buried alive? Everything's changed, Wheat ... except my memory.'

'You were hanged. You couldn't ...' Cater was morbidly interested, but fearful of the words.

'I *could*. Most o' you were too damn cowardly to watch, or had ridden off. I had a knife. That tight corsetry weren't all bones ... not ever. I managed to cut the rope. For a while I was free.' Cater's legs were unsteady, and he backed off to the edge of his table. 'What do you mean?'

'One o' you came back. I couldn't see his face.' Ida Rose took a step into the office. Cater flinched, but Ida stayed near the door, as if to guard her way out. 'I was lyin' in a crumpled heap, but he still shot me. It was the darkest night, but he was sure he'd killed me. He dragged me, rolled me over a cutbank. He wanted all that goddamn river stuff to eat me.'

'But, you got out ... away?'

'Yeah. Took as long as it took my hair to turn the colour of a bighorn's scut. I was hurt bad with the bullet wounds.'

'Why so long before comin' back?'

'I wanted the anger to go. But I'm tired o' waitin'.'

Cater felt vulnerable. 'Jesus, Ida. We sorta thought your girls would come to get you. Why'd any one of us come back an' deliberately shoot, then try an' drown you?' he asked.

'I was just the top hand o' the Rosado,' Ida said slowly. 'The one who came back was the leader. He tried to kill me because he feared I might talk.'

'How could he have known you weren't dead?'

'He didn't. He was just nervous of me *not* bein'. He'd've been another snapper meal if my tongue took to waggin'.'

'That don't make sense, Ida. What's the point in him—'

'You can call your friends out now,' Ida interrupted Cater's question.

Holstering their guns, Rufus and Eady stepped back into the office.

Ida Rose considered them with an icy stare. 'I've seen you before,' she said.

'An' I've seen *you*,' Eady answered. 'The three of us were sittin' at table in Longfield's dinin' room. You didn't stay long, I recall. I'm Eady Dix, this is Rufus Breese.'

'It's *you* I remember. You're kind o' curious . . . sort o' sticks in the mind.'

'Are you back ridin' with the Rosado?' Rufus cut across the line of talk.

'If you've been listenin', what the hell do *you* think?' Ida directed back at him. 'I hear they're up an' runnin' though.'

Then, with her blue eyes still holding the three in the office, the one-time madam of Quemadero's one-time cathouse, backed towards the door that led to the alley. The door opened and closed, and without another word, or seeming to move much, Ida Rose was gone.

'That's the second time she's done that,' Eady said. 'It's somethin' we could all learn from.' For a

113

moment or two there was no sound, save the soft spluttering of the lamp on Cater's desk. Then the wall thudded, as the rattled saloon keeper kicked his chair against it.

A moment later, the shocking blast of a gun resounded in the alley, and their eyes darted back to the door. The door flew open, and once again, Ida Rose was standing there. But this time, her face was held in a taut grimace. She staggered forward and Eady groaned and rushed towards her.

'They ain't my girls,' Ida gasped. Then her eyes locked painfully into Eady's. 'We waste so much,' she added enigmatically, almost inaudibly. Then she pitched forward, her slender body sprawled on the floor's dust-layered carpet.

Rufus leaped to the open door. With his Colt drawn, he half stepped into the darkness of the alley. There was no one there, but he thought he heard something, and a breeze stirred the chilly air.

Eady was kneeling beside Ida's body. 'I think I know what you mean,' she said. 'But if we find 'em for you, I promise it won't be *everythin'* wasted.' Then she looked up, and the words caught in her throat. 'They've struck her, Rufe. An' I think she was walkin' away.'

Rufus didn't say anything. He looked down, stared hard, as the blood oozed darkly across the back of Ida's long ribbon shirt.

18

THE FALLEN
WOMAN

Anger and frustration swept over Eady as she stared
at the still figure of Ida Rose. Wheat Cater scowled.
His features looked heavy and sweaty in the yellow
light as he let himself fall heavily into his chair.

'I'll help you find 'em,' he said. 'I owe her that.'

'You sure as hell do,' Eady agreed sullenly.

'An' we ain't overlookin' the fact that you still *could*
be a leader o' the Rosado,' Rufus pointed out.

Cater glared back defiantly. 'Ida gettin' plugged
like that sorta proves I ain't, don't it?'

'Not really. Just maybe,' Eady said, thoughtfully.

'More's the pity,' an overbearing voice growled
from the alley door. With two of his gunslicks in the
alley behind him, Barton Frimley stood watching.
Then he stepped into Cater's office, his men moving

forward to either side of the door.

'I'd like to meet someone that knows he *is*,' Eady said, her voice full of weighed-up meaning.

'If you're meanin' *me*, lady. . . .' Frimley said, threateningly. 'I ain't forgettin' what happened out at the Twist.'

'Nor have we,' Rufus answered back. 'But I ain't bruisin' any more fingerbones on your thick skull. I told you what would happen the next time we met, Frimley. An' right now would be the worst ever o' times. Believe me.'

At that, Eady stood up very slowly. She looked hard at Frimley, was daring him to make a move.

'Ha,' Frimley sneered. 'None o' you are in a position to threaten anybody.'

'An' you ain't goin' to shoot all three of us,' Cater spoke up. 'If either o' these two goes down, the other one'll get you. An' if *they* don't, *I will*,' he warned.

'How the hell you goin' to do that, Cater? Goin' to gob some baccy juice at me? I know where you keep that rifle o' yours.'

'Yep. Right above your head. But under this desk, there's a big Walker Colt. That's sixty grains o' black powder pointin' at your gut. One o' your men pulls a trigger, an' they'll have to bury you in pieces.'

Before anyone could respond, Rufus intervened. 'You can live another day without fightin' for it,' he offered Frimley. 'All you got to do is walk away.'

With an angry gesture, Frimley wiped away a gobbet of spit from his mouth, regarded Rufus with loathing in his eyes. Then he sighed, shrugged and turned, looked like he was heeding Rufus. But, as he brushed past one of his gunmen, his right hand quickly snatched the man's Colt from its holster.

The men were surprised, momentarily distracted. Eady, though, had seen and was ready for Frimley's chicanery. She drew her Colt, and before Frimley had a chance to put a bullet into Rufus, he was staggering backwards, collapsing with two bullets tearing his chest apart.

Rufus took one long, deep breath. 'I got that all wrong,' he said, staring through the door out at Frimley's bloody body. 'For a moment there, I thought we had someone actually takin' my advice.'

Cater moved forward and pulled down the Winchester he kept above the door. He levered a shell into the breech, was itching for a target. He glared at the two gunmen. 'Anythin', an' you die,' he said, without trace of emotion.

Eady stepped between them, a cold glitter in her eyes. 'Was Frimley one o' the Rosados'?' she demanded. 'I'll shoot you dead if you say no.'

'Yeah, he was one of 'em,' the man said.

Eady nodded. 'Was he the boss?'

'No,' the other gunman said quickly. 'He got his orders an' passed 'em down.'

'Who's the big enchilada handin' out pretty garters then?' Eady pressured.

'Why the hell should we know or care? We work for the money, not the grudge.'

Rufus had just decided that more reprisals weren't necessary when the inside door of Cater's office was hammered by someone's fist.

'Is that you in there, Wheat?' called a voice that Rufus and Eady thought they recognized. 'What's all that goddamn shootin'?'

Rufus nodded at Cater, who went to the inner door and unlocked it. He pulled it open, confronted Clovis Finn who was standing there with the saloon's callous barkeep.

'What the hell!' the card player exclaimed, looking around quickly.

'We had us some trouble,' Cater said. 'You'd never know it, but that's Ida Rose. Frimley's outside.'

'Ida Rose?' Finn repeated. 'She came back? That hell-born actually came back here?'

'Yeah, but it weren't for long. Somebody back-shot her.'

'An' they shot Frimley?' the barkeep wanted to know.

'No, *I did*,' Eady said. 'He was a liar, a cheat an' a coward . . . a miserable cur. Oh, an' a Rosado.'

'Who was headin' 'em up? Who's leadin' 'em now?' Finn asked.

'It weren't Ida Rose. Nor Frimley.'

'That's too bad,' Finn reflected grimly.

19

RETURNING GUNS

In less than ten minutes from Eady's shooting of Barton Frimley, Yule Arnold appeared with the Tucumcari deputies. Pentland Betts and Ogden Rimsayle were in meddlesome, close attendance.

'I know what you're thinkin',' Rufus muttered to Eady, as the group jostled in the doorway.

'Time to rob the rest o' the town,' Eady voiced, on the brink of loudness.

Arnold pushed his way. He was carrying an aged scattergun, scowled as he saw Cater's Winchester covering the two gunmen.

'I shoulda known it was you two,' he grated, on seeing Rufus and Eady. 'I suppose you'll be wantin' stars next. What's happened?'

Cater quickly explained the last ten minutes.

'Well there's nothin' in any o' that that convinces me that these two aren't the Rosado leaders,'

Rimsayle snorted. 'What about the Tomkiss note, an' the garter that was found on 'em? This town needs smarter law enforcement, an' I'll be puttin' that forward at the next election.'

'Ah shut up, you pompous windbag,' Cater yelled at Rimsayle. 'None of us wants to listen to you.'

'*You* shut up,' Rimsayle bellowed back. 'You don't rule this town yet. These two broke jail, an' I want to know who helped 'em.'

'I did,' Cater said calmly. 'I gave 'em a gun, an' warned 'em to get out of town . . . anywhere away from you . . . you an' Finn's lynch mob.'

'That's a goddamn lie,' snapped Finn.

'I've heard enough,' Arnold said, and grinned at Eady. 'I *would* have come after you, if I'd thought you guilty.'

'Yeah, I know it, Sheriff.' Eady attempted a smile, and eased her Colt back into the holster.

Arnold then looked at Rufus. 'I figured that you an' her would learn a lot more'n me,' he said. 'An' you did. You found Ida Rose, an' you found out that Frimley was in league with the Rosado.'

'Yeah, well, you're nearly right. The lady found us,' Rufus corrected him.

Arnold nodded thoughtfully, told the deputies to take Frimley's gunmen off to the jail. 'An' someone take charge o' the bodies,' he said to no one in particular.

For a short while, and undeterred, Ogden Rimsayle continued to bicker. Finn was suddenly gone and no one else was interested. Rimsayle snorted his disgust and stomped from the office towards the main street.

'Next time the territory has an armed get-together, I hope it finds somewhere bigger than my office,' Cater said wryly. 'An' now, Sheriff, some of us have got a round-up to go to.'

'Not until first light,' Rufus added.

Pentland Betts was already backing off through the door. 'I was wonderin' if anyone would think o' that,' he said, spat his dark dribble on to the boardwalk. He walked off into the darkness, said he'd try for a few hours' undisturbed sleep.

Eady tossed Cater's revolver on to the desk, leaned her back tiredly against the wall. 'I'd like to have my own gun back, Sheriff,' she said. 'An' Rufus.'

Arnold gave Rufus a sly glance. 'Stop by the office to collect 'em. I'd hate to pull the trigger on this ol' cannon. It ain't ever fired anythin' but crook nails.'

Rufus glanced at the sheriff's empty holster and grinned, handed over the .45. 'Thanks for the use,' he said.

Eady suddenly held up her hand for attention, nodded in the direction of hoofs drumming along the street. 'Sounds like important work,' she said. 'I wonder where it's at?'

'They're too far in the van for us to catch 'em,' Rufus responded.

Arnold got keen. 'But we could sure goddamn try,' he said.

'That's more like it, Sheriff,' Cater said with a wry grin. 'Let's round up every man we can get . . . meet the trouble that's surely comin'. If we're attackin' in defence, the Rosados'll surely be doin' the same.'

'Bearin' that in mind, what's the best way to gather a crowd that ain't still leanin' towards neck-tie parties?' Arnold enquired.

'Send one o' your deputies to the Ancho Arena an' another over to see Lyman Hench,' Rufus replied. 'Tell 'em what's happened . . . to be ready for trouble.'

'An' to stand off, else they'll probably get shot as a messenger,' Eady added.

'I'll wake up every man in town that can be trusted. Allow me five minutes,' Cater said, with a dry smile. 'What about you an' Eady, Rufus?'

'Collect our horses from Betts, pick up our guns from the sheriff's office, an' head for the Barley Parcel. That's where we're reckonin' on the HQ o' the Rosado bein'.'

'An' you'll give a warnin' if they head this way? You'll find some way to stop the ironclad here from sailin' in?'

'Can't guarantee *that*,' Rufus said. 'Of late, we been puttin' up a united front.'

'I can think o' worse things,' Cater responded with an appreciative smile.

The four then separated. The sheriff went to give orders to his deputies, and Cater set off to rouse the few townsmen he trusted.

Rufus and Eady hurried to the livery stable. But the place was locked and deserted. When they pounded on the door there was no answer.

'He must have a vital appointment somewhere,' Rufus said.

'Yeah, an' *we* must have our horses,' Eady insisted.

20

RAILROAD DEAL

Rufus and Eady hurried around to the rear of the stable. The back door was closed, so Rufus took one step back and lashed out with his boot heel.

'I wonder what Arnold's fine is for destruction o' property?' Eady muttered, as the door gave way.

Inside, there was an oil lantern burning, but most of the stable was in the gloom. From the stalls, a horse kicked, jerked nervously at its strap line.

'Excited by the company,' Rufus observed. 'There's nobody else here.'

Eady and Rufus got their horses from the stalls, saddled them up, and led them out through the back door that was hanging off its hinges.

'Where'd we find the Barley Parcel?' Rufus wanted to know, as he swung up into the saddle. 'Where the others ain't, I guess. Must be somewhere west o' here,' Eady said.

From collecting their Colts at the sheriff's office, they rode west to pick up the wagon road. They'd gone a mile past the town's grave patch, when they were approached by a rider who'd been waiting for them in the shade of a seep-willow.

'Ease up. Leave this one to me,' Rufus said, sensing Eady's tautness.

'You know what happened to the half-bake who last pulled this sort o' stunt?' he rasped, at the man who held ground in front of them.

Stub Jessel held a rifle alongside his right leg. 'Well, I'm *fully baked*, an' nothin's happenin' to *me*,' he crowed.

'There's another reason why this ain't your lucky day, Jessel.'

'Yeah, why's that?'

'It's the day I finally had it with people pullin' guns on me . . . tellin' me to move on,' Rufus blasted back. 'Now, if you got the sand, go ahead . . . try for a shot.'

There was a short, intense wait, then Jessel's eyes gave him away. They flickered, moved a fraction to his right, as Eady flipped the reins of her bayo.

It was all that Rufus needed. He drew and put a bullet straight into Jessel's chest, then another, fast, as the body jerked in the saddle.

Jessel looked futilely at Rufus. His eyes tried to blink away the confusion and the pain. His arms and fingers turned numb and he couldn't get off the shot he desperately wanted to. 'You're right . . . it ain't,' he gasped, and let go of his rifle, took a final, short gulp of air and followed it to the dirt.

Rufus watched, sat waiting for the fall. He thrust his gun back into the holster and swung out of the saddle. It took a moment, nothing more than a hasty glance to know that Jessel was dead.

Eady complimented Rufus on his work. 'You'll soon be as good as me with that hogleg,' she said.

'His time was run out,' Rufus said. 'There'd never have been a next time.'

But there was no need for an explanation. Eady knew the treacherous character of Emile Rednapp's ex-foreman. 'What now?' she asked. 'We still headin' for the Barley Parcel?'

'Yeah. After I take care o' this.'

Rufus dragged the body to the side of the road. 'Pretty straightforward way to die. That's rare in these parts,' he said harshly. Jessel's mount had wandered over to the side of the road, and it stood there waiting, its dark coat shiny in the looming darkness. Rufus picked up the reins and tied them loosely to the saddle horn. He gave the animal a slap on its flank and it trotted away, headed for the corral at Ancho Arena.

'Doubt they'll send out a rider.' Rufus was almost dismissive. He remounted and together they continued riding west along the wagon road.

'Do you think Jessel was out for *us*?' Rufus asked after a few minutes.

'No. Not you an' me personal. He was here to protect whoever it was rode from town. He would've shot anyone chasin' 'em.'

'Well, *we* know what *they* do,' Rufus suggested.

126

'That the ranchers are gettin' ready to fight back.'

'Yeah, an' the stories of Ida Rose an' Barton Frimley.'

'There's one thing for certain, Eady. Whatever Rednapp's problem with Jessel, it ain't any more.'

'No. Not that Rednapp knows it,' Eady said. 'I wonder if Jessel was a member of the Rosado?' she added.

'If he wasn't, I just made him an honorary one.' Rufus pointed to the west, and they left the wagon road, headed towards the Barley Parcel.

'How does all this tie in with that railroad deal, Rufe?' Eady asked thoughtfully. 'Because there's *nothin'* else makes much sense.'

'Yeah, I'm beginnin' to think the same,' Rufus said. 'The Barley Parcel's *big*, but it ain't nothin' more'n the original parcel . . . not in the same league as the others. If that rail spur does run from Albuquerque, it'll go through land that's owned by Dancer, Rednapp and Hench . . . *not* Frimley's. They'll bend south to Fort Sumner or even Farwell before that.'

'An' that means no settlement money for Mr Frimley, as opposed to an ungodly mountain of it, if he'd owned—'

'—the land that he didn't,' Rufus jumped in eagerly. 'But him bein' Rosado's top hand did help him right along in gettin' it.'

The land began to change as they moved further west. Towards the tail end of the Sangre de Cristos, the land became more severe, with isolated mesas and dry, gravelly washes. It was from around the low wall of one of these gullies that the riders appeared. There were five of them, and they had an assortment of garments wound loose around their faces and upper bodies. They were all armed and they weren't speaking or exchanging commands. The concern for Rufus and Eady was the way they spread as they rode forward.

'Hey! Did you mean it when you said we go where each other goes?' Eady asked.

Rufus narrowed his eyes at the riders ahead. 'Yeah, an' how could I have been that stupid,' he said.

21

THE BOSS MAN

Accepting the certain chance of getting blasted from their saddles before they cleared leather, neither Rufus nor Eady made an attempt on their guns. They sat waiting, as the horsemen surrounded them in continued, menacing silence.

One of the men rode close to Rufus's right, reached out and drew his Colt from the holster. Another, who'd edged his horse to Eady, did the same.

'I know her,' one of the shrouded men said, eventually. 'She's the gunny. Her name's Eady Dix. There's an old border Jehu knows her as "Britches", or some such.'

'It was her that shot Frimley,' said the man who'd taken Rufus's gun.

'Is that a good or bad move for us?' Rufus asked him.

The man didn't answer. But another said for them all to move out. 'Someone's goin' to be real pleased to see these two,' he said.

That news meant that Rufus and Eady would be safe, at least until they got to the Barley Parcel. Rufus closed his eyes, dropped his chin and let the sabino walk on. He didn't look back, but guessed Eady was probably doing similar. After all, there wasn't much for them to talk about.

But it was raised voices that snapped Rufus from his deadpan reverie. He looked up to see the shapes of low buildings huddled in the darkness ahead, realized they'd reached Barton Frimley's ranch. He noticed all the horses in the corrals, many more than an outfit working on a ranch this size would be needing. Lights gleamed through the windows of the main building and the bunkhouse had yellow squares that cut the night.

'Horses doin' their own late dealin', are they?' he said insolently.

'You let your mouth work, mister,' one of the riders answered. 'It ain't goin' to last much longer.'

The seven riders reached the front of the ranch house and halted their mounts. A harsh-featured man stepped from the front doorway. 'What you brought us tonight?' he asked.

'A couple o' mavericks,' said one of the masked riders, as he swung down from his horse. 'The boss'll know 'em. Is he here?'

'Yeah,' said the man on the porch. 'I'll see if he wants 'em pushed on through.'

For a minute, Rufus and Eady sat quietly, each of them pondering on their fate, assessing the chances of survival.

'The boss is feelin' hospitable. Says you two are to come on in,' the man said, on returning. 'You other men saddle up fresh horses. Be ready to ride in an hour.'

'We guardin' another goddamn road?' one of the men near the steps asked.

'No. You're ridin' to Quemadero,' said the man standing above them. 'Now, bring on them Frimley killers.'

Mindful of the men around them, Rufus and Eady swung from their saddles. They let their reins fall, warily eyed the two men who stood near them.

With Eady by his side, Rufus started up the veranda steps. He stopped for a short moment, his interest stirred when he saw all the horses bar one being led to the nearby corral. When they crossed the veranda, the man in the doorway took a long look out into the dark distance. Then he took a slow step back as they entered the lighted hallway.

Towards the rear of the house, there was a half-open door. Rufus went up to it, stopped outside the small, book-lined study.

A man was sitting at a leather-topped writing desk. In the light from an oil lamp's engraved shade, he held his hands beneath the desk. It instantly reminded Rufus of Wheat Cater and the big Walker Colt.

'I wondered what happened to you,' Rufus said, looking distastefully at Clovis Finn.

131

*

Rufus recalled Wheat Cater saying that it was Finn, together with Rimsayle, who were shouting for the necks of him and Eady. He thought he'd better create less offence.

From the chair, Finn looked past Rufus, up at the harsh-featured man who'd been standing on the veranda. 'You know the orders, Polk,' he said. 'Go an' close Quemadero.'

'Sure thing,' the man called Polk said. Then he turned to leave with the two guards whose faces were still concealed.

Finn, noticed the fading smile on Rufus's face. 'Pleased because you ain't dead yet?' he asked.

'No. It's because I don't reckon you're the one who's really givin' the orders here.'

'Huh, that's as maybe,' Finn said, with a lean, cheerless smile. 'Why don't you an' Miss Dix come in? Perhaps we can all talk peckin' orders.'

Rufus realized then that there was another man in the room with Finn. He was sitting on the end of a stub sofa, had a walnut-stocked scattergun across his knees. He was also wearing a hangman's cowl, and Rufus shuddered.

'You two don't seem to appreciate when to hitch a ride, 'cause that would have been my advice,' Finn said, looking at Eady as he spoke. 'Now look at the mess you got yourselves in.'

Strangely, the first thing that Eady thought of was Finn's interest in Beth Longfield. The man was a

132

gambler, and he'd obviously been playing for her hand. So, revealing his hand as the leader of a bunch of land thieves and murderers, was surely a very bad call and to be avoided. Eady thought that was good advice, and a good riposte, but she held it in.

Eady edged closer to Rufus, but with a low raspy voice, the other man called for her to stay where she was.

'You got out here fast,' Rufus said to Finn. 'You weren't that far ahead of us . . . *when you left town.*'

Suddenly, Finn looked uneasy. 'Yeah, that was me. I had to go lookin' for her,' he said. He started to say something else, but the other man told him to shut up.

A bemused Rufus and Eady then heard the dull pounding of horses' hoofs. It was from the front yard, and they guessed it would be the Rosado heading off for Quemadero.

A pang of guilt thumped at Rufus, as he remembered telling Wheat Cater and the sheriff that they'd warn the town if the Rosado was on its way.

Eady cast a troubled look from the masked man to Finn. 'I'd feel a whole lot less nervy if you got them paws on the table,' she said. 'I got reason to distrust fellers who sit like that.'

Finn thought for a moment, then brought up his hands. 'You got nothin' to worry about,' he said, turning his wrists to show the cord binding.

22

THE GETAWAY

It was the hooded man who got to his feet. 'I warned you not to play this some other way,' he rasped, finding it hard to retain his whisper.

'Huh, it don't make the difference,' Rufus said, staring at Finn's bound wrists. 'We got you tagged as nothin' more'n a sergeant. No, it's the ghoul standin' there with a goddamn flour bag on his head. He's the one we want. The ugly son-of-a-bitch has to keep his face covered for fear of ever passin' a mirror. Ha, that's a bit o' funnin' we had with one or two of his dragoons, before they died.'

The hooded man's pale eyes bore chillingly into Rufus. They could almost hear the grind of his jaw. It was a moment of trigger tension and nobody paid much attention to Eady. She'd edged off a step, and they didn't see her reach inside a hanging fold of her buckskin coat and draw a Colt.

134

'There's times when bein' a woman comes in real handy,' she said, with a mischievous smile. 'Now, drop the scattergun,' she snapped at the hooded man.

The man saw the dogged set of Eady's face. He grunted and drooped the big barrels of his gun. But only so far. Taking advantage of the split second of surprise, he swung an arm and smashed the oil lamp with the shotgun. In the immediate and intense darkness, it dashed across the floor towards Rufus's feet.

Eady dropped to the floor with the expected blast of gunfire resounding madly in the close confines of the room. She knew the man would keep the second barrel for a second chance if he needed it. Then she saw the man's shape filling the window opening as he went through and away. She fired, knowing it was too late, too difficult a shot.

A moment later they all heard the thump of boots along the front veranda. Then excited snorting, the hoofbeats of the roan that had remained in the yard.

'That's the Rosado chief, the man you're all after,' came Finn's voice from the darkness. 'He'll be dippin' his toes into the Conchas lake before mid-mornin'.'

Eady found her way to the door. She went out to the hall to fetch an oil lamp, brought it back into the den. She still had the gun in her other hand, and she dropped it into her empty holster.

'Where the hell did *that* come from?' Rufus asked her.

'Frimley. He lifted it from one of his gunmen: lifted it from *him* in the alley . . . thought it might come in handy.'

'Yeah, good thinkin',' Rufus muttered. He took the lamp and placed it on the desk, pulled out a clasp-knife and cut the ropes that bound Clovis Finn's wrists.

'Frimley had Beth Longfield taken, didn't he?' Eady put to Finn. 'That's why you rode lickety-split from town. It was to go lookin' for her.'

'Yeah,' Finn said, rubbing the soreness of his wrists. 'She weren't anywhere at the house. I found that out after I left you at the Tall Top.'

'You got any ideas about our lost friend?' Rufus asked speculatively. 'Did he say or do *anythin'* ? Somethin' you could finger him with?'

Finn shook his head. 'No, nothin'. But funny thing is; one minute I got a bead on him, next minute it disappears like the spectre he's meant to be. We must know him though, otherwise he would-n't have that whispery voice when he speaks, which ain't much.'

'There's somethin got me thinkin', too, Rufe,' Eady said. 'I don't know what, but it's somethin'. I reckon Finn's right, we *do* know him.'

'Oh, we know him all right,' Rufus said, shook his head with frustration.

'So, are we gettin' the hell out o' this place?' Finn said. 'I don't want to be here when them killer spooks come back, 'cause they will.'

Rufus went over to a high cabinet that was fitted in

one corner of the room. He turned a key and pulled open the double doors. 'Here,' he said, looking at the revolvers and rifles stacked inside. 'It's a sort o' Christmas. Help yourself.'

Eady agreed. She selected one of a pair of .44 Army Colts and stuffed it behind the buckle of her belt.

Finn picked up a smaller .36 revolver, examined it, and thrust it into a shoulder holster he wore beneath his coat. 'Maybe they brought Beth *here*,' he said eagerly.

'Why the hell didn't you mention it before?' Eady flashed out. 'Where will she be?'

'I don't think she'd be anywhere down here.'

They went quickly back into the hall and looked around them, out through the open doorway. There was no movement and, bristling with firearms, the three of them ran up the stairs to the upper floor.

Wall sconces that burned at the head of the stairway threw eerie shadows around them. At the end of a broad corridor, a door stood open and more light came from the room beyond.

They all walked directly to the door, peered into a bedroom where Beth was lying on the bed. Her hands and feet were tied, her hair was tousled and her face was tearfully wet.

Eady pushed into the room. 'Sorry we're late, Beth,' she said with a comforting smile. 'Mister Finn was tied up, else he woulda been here.'

Finn gave Eady a trying look. He stepped in quickly and untied the ropes, drew them carefully away from Beth's wrists and ankles.

'How'd they get you, Beth?' he asked.

Beth sat up on the bed, swung her legs to the ground. 'I was out doin' the scrap bins . . . leftovers for Dalmyer's hogs. They must have been waitin'. They tied me up an' put me on a blanket in the back of a buck-wagon. I kept my eyes shut . . . didn't know where we were goin'. I'm so pleased to see you all . . . you, Clovis,' she said.

Finn smiled and gripped her shoulder lightly. Rufus and Eady shared an understanding look.

After a long moment, Rufus wanted conformation of something. 'You couldn't see who they were, could you?' he said.

Beth shook her head. 'No. Their heads were covered.'

'I think we should be makin' a move,' Eady decided.

Finn agreed. Beth pushed herself from the bed and Rufus had a quick look from the window.

'If any o' them Rosados' are Comanche renegades, they could be out there waitin' an' you wouldn't know it,' he said.

Before leaving, the four of them allowed a few disturbing thoughts to settle. Then from downstairs, a door slammed into its frame.

'They're inside.' Eady turned to Rufus, but he was ahead of her, already at the head of the stairs.

'It's the goddamn oil . . . from the lamp,' he said. He pulled his gun and started down the stairs, pumping bullets into the darkness below.

Then the flames appeared. First, small yellow waves that licked at the wood, then a fiercer cloud of red and gold.

'They're burnin' us out,' Rufus yelled. 'Get down here fast.'

23

BURNED OUT

On the ground floor now, the flames spread quickly as they overwhelmed the oil-soaked floor. They rolled around the foot of the stairs, found a route and crawled upward.

But Rufus, Eady, Beth and Clovis Finn were down and away, through the big parlour doors at the back of the house.

'Did you see sign of anyone?' Rufus asked Eady, as for a moment they looked back at the burning.

'Not a ghost,' Eady said. 'That door bangin' was them leavin'.'

'Yeah. Let's go see if the horses are still here,' Rufus recommended.

They ran for the harness shed, which was far enough from the house not to be in any danger of catching a flying ember. They found saddles, all the other rigging they needed and, when they reached the corral, Eady was more relieved.

'Our horses are here, Rufe. Just as we left 'em,' she called out.

Rufus roped a horse apiece for Beth and Finn, then they gathered their gear and saddled up.

Rufus looked determinedly at Eady. 'Sometime soon, those dogs'll put one, or both of us, into the ground,' he said. 'So let's be the wind up *their* asses for a change.'

'That's a sound, martial argument,' Rufe,' Eady said, already moving off her bayo as she swung into the saddle.

They rode from the corral, and Rufus made a loop to leave the gate wide open. The horses balked, as the back end of the house's roof gave way, and the ammunition beneath the gun cabinet went up. They snorted, flicked their legs, went into an excited run, and the riders gave them their heads.

After they'd raced more than two miles in the direction of Quemadero, the horses slowed to a steady trot.

'You still carryin' the time?' Rufus asked.

'Nearly three,' Eady said, without lookin' at the hunter.

They rode in silence, and an hour later the buildings of Quemadero emerged as dark outlines. It was an early hour, but there was no sign of movement in the town.

'That's strange. I was certain they were comin' here tonight,' Rufus said.

Finn closed his horse alongside Rufus's sabino.

'You were there when I told Polk to shut the town up?' he said.

'Yeah, words to that effect. But you never meant it,' Rufus answered.

'*They* didn't know that.'

'There's lamps burnin' in my place,' Beth said.

Slow and quiet, they rode into the deserted main street, reined in outside of the Longfield. They all dismounted, Rufus and Eady loose tying their mares to the hitching rail.

Beth and Finn led the way up and into the lobby where the oil lamps had been turned low. Beth's night clerk was dozing at the desk, and he was taken aback, looked wretched.

Wheat Cater hailed them as they came in. 'Hey, they let you through.' He advanced on them, grinning with relief. His Winchester was clutched tight in his nervy hands.

'Who let us through? Where?' Rufus asked.

Cater said, 'They've got us nailed down tighter than a harpy's coffin. Those that try an' leave, get shot.'

'How many?'

'Three, up until now.'

'So, who've we got in town?' Eady asked.

'Not many, if I get your meanin'.'

Rufus turned to look back through the door. 'How about walkin' the street?' he asked Cater.

'They ain't tried anythin' out there yet.'

Eady looked from Beth to Finn, then back at Cater. 'Don't forget Arnold's deputies. They should have warned Rednapp an' Hench by now. If there's no trouble out there, they'll be back.'

'We ain't forgettin', Eady. It's just that right now, we ain't feelin' too optimistic about anythin' much,' Cater said.

Rufus looked at the eager faces. 'Come daybreak, we'll get an idea o' their layout . . . their weak points,' he said hopefully.

'Hmm. That's somethin' to look forward to,' Cater muttered drily.

'Well, we ain't in any danger this moment,' Eady suggested. 'So why don't some of us get our heads down.'

Finn waved his arm out towards the stairs. 'Yeah, you go, Beth, you deserve it,' he said. 'I'll bring Wheat up to date.'

'An' we'll take care o' the horses,' Eady said.

Out front, Rufus and Eady swung back into their saddles, took the reins of the other two horses from Finn.

'Stay out o' trouble,' Rufus said, and the pair rode off towards the livery stable.

'Open up, Betts. You can pretend you dreamed the whole thing,' Rufus shouted, through the narrow, side door of the livery stable.

Inside, Betts got lazily to his feet. The front door opened after a while, and Rufus and Eady rode their horses through.

'Leave 'em there, I'll take care o' the unsaddlin',' Betts said. 'I want you gone an' that's the truth of it.

You're both trouble . . . it's treadin' your tails.'

Rufus shrugged and left the stable with Eady, headed back towards the Longfield. It was a scary, nerve jangling walk, knowing that armed killers were waiting in the darkness.

'You still tryin' to fit a face on the Rosado?' Rufus asked.

'Yeah, I am, Goddamnit, he's so familiar, I can almost smell him,' Eady said. 'He was the one who came back an' set fire to the Barley Parcel, wasn't he?'

'Yeah, that was him,' Rufus said.

They walked on in silence, had almost reached the Longfield, when a figure loomed from the shadows. Yule Arnold stood solid on the boardwalk in front of them.

'Christ, that's a reckless place to take in the air,' Eady gasped, her Colt already in her hand. 'You could be breathin' through the top o' your head.'

'Where'd you two spring from?' the sheriff demanded officiously.

'The livery. Why?' Rufus asked, pushing his own Colt back.

'Them Rosados have got the town surrounded. We're all penned down. Prior to what, only varmints an' Lucifer hisself knows.'

'That's a tad dramatic, Sheriff, but yeah, we know the score.'

'I took this Quemadero post 'cause it was civic,' Arnold said, his manner tired and already half beat. 'I left the fight in Tucumcari. Now my brain an' body's too slow . . .'

'Then leave it to us,' Rufus proposed. 'If it goes belly-up, we'll form circles an' play checkers . . . wait for your deputies to bring reinforcements.'

24

THE BARRICADE

The three of them went straight to the jailhouse. Once inside, the sheriff locked the door and drew the blinds. He lit two hanging oil lamps and motioned Rufus and Eady to a pair of spoke-back chairs.

'Now, tell me what's been happenin',' he said, having seated himself at his desk.

Rufus briefly explained how they'd been captured and taken to Frimley's ranch. How they'd found Clovis Finn being forced to act as the leader of the Rosado, while under the threat of a shotgun. He told of Beth Longfield and of how they'd escaped, of the man who'd come back to burn the ranch house down around them.

Arnold was stunned. 'An' you reckon he's their leader? He rode back here . . . to Quemadero?' he asked.

'Yeah, we're sure of it. He's scuttlin' through a rat run somewhere,' Rufus said. 'But bringin' him in's no longer your problem – that's the way you want it?'

'Just tell me . . . *us*, what to do to help.'

Rufus nodded his acknowledgement of the sheriff's co-operation, started on his quickly considered advice. 'In an hour, we'll be into daylight. Get everyone up an' on to the street. Roll out some wagons an' carts to build a barricade. Use anythin'.'

'They'll come in from the west end o' town, so we'll put some men with guns across the street,' Eady chipped in. 'Give these sidewinders some *real* blood-red garters. An' if you've got a dog, *bring it*, get it to bark.'

'I'll see all that gets done,' Arnold said.

Quickly and efficiently, they all went from building to building along the street, rousing folk, telling them what was to be done. No one argued, and soon there was all manner of weaponry behind all manner of mercantile and domestic wares. Through one or two trapdoored ceilings, some men were staked-out on the rooftops.

Rufus and Eady and the sheriff took a break from their allotted tasks. They stood on the boardwalk, looked over the defences.

'They'll see it, an' turn back,' Arnold, groused.

'No, just slow 'em down for us. These are civic improvements, for cuttin' out through traffic,' Rufus said, with a grim, uncertain smile.

'You got your people in place?' Eady asked Arnold.

'Best I can, yeah.'

147

'That's good, Sheriff, because this'll be them comin' now. Welcome to a new day, one an' all.'

Ten minutes after first light broke on to the land between the Pecos and Canadian rivers, a band of shrouded horsemen arrived at the western end of the town. The last of Rufus Breese's shouted instructions were lost as the muffled rumble of more than twenty horses swept around the dog-leg, raced for the makeshift barricade. They were in a skirmish line, their stirrups almost touching, and each man brandished a rifle.

'Aim low . . . fire!' Rufus shouted, when the riders were less than thirty yards away.

On his words, the first volley of gunfire from the town's defenders roared out. The smoke and stench of cordite swirled around them as flames stabbed from nearly a dozen guns. But Eady held her fire. She was peering through a gap in the barricade, while Rufus showed her that three men had already crashed from their saddles. Then Rufus called for another broadside, watched intently as another man fell.

With Eady following, Rufus then ran for the boardwalk where Wheat Cater was standing in the half light. He'd taken shelter behind one of the supports of an overhang, and Rufus and Eady took up kneeling positions.

'We got to stop meetin' like this,' Eady yelled at Cater.

'Why?' the saloon keeper yelled back, with a

welcoming grin.

The wild pounding of hoofs, the shouting and cursing of fighting men, the stench of cordite, the flashes of flame and the roaring of the shooting, merged to a bedlam. From the far side of the street, a large grey dog stood splay-legged on the boardwalk. It barked loudly and frantically, its head pointing to the sky, black eyes bulging.

Rufus understood. All the wild sounds seemed unreal and far away. For a short moment he'd become detached, laughed at the dog as if he was no longer involved in the fight.

Then he was aware of the attackers' horses closing on the barricade. He cursed as two of the defenders took fatal bullets. He saw someone crawling towards the boardwalk, bleeding bad from head and shoulder wounds. Another was stretched out flailing the dust, wouldn't likely get up again.

Then, the surging line of horses was leaping the barricade.

The firing was point blank, and the Rosados were using six-guns. Rufus knew they'd be counting on a single attack, expecting the defenders' resistance to be short-lived. Whoever was leading them was plainly going for the breakthrough.

Eady started shooting as the first of the horsemen leapt the barricade. She saw her man go down, and that Rufus was firing steadily. Cater was gritting his teeth as he hard-worked the action of his Winchester.

Two men made a dash for the boardwalk, and

Rufus sent one of them down with a bullet that almost lifted away his hood. For a split second it looked as if Clovis Finn was about to meet his end, but he ducked as the bullets crashed out from Eady's Colt. Rufus leaped, clutching low at the second attacker's legs. He knew one of them was going to die, rolled striking and kicking as they went down. Then Eady took aim and shot the man almost point blank.

'Had to. Beth would never forgive me,' she said.

Breathing hard, Finn straightened up. He spluttered some gratitude and took shelter with Rufus.

'You're right, Eady,' Rufus shouted. 'Gettin' good's just a matter o' practice.'

The last of the hooded men were fighting for control, dragging their mounts around in tight circles. They were desperately firing at the men behind the barricade, stationed along the boardwalk, up at those who'd got vantage points on the rooftops. There were many riderless horses, and the Rosado were no longer fighting with the wrath or order they'd displayed when they'd first galloped down the street.

'We're scarin' 'em,' Yule Arnold yelled.

'They ain't the only ones,' Rufus shouted back, as he started a reload.

At that moment, and from the same, western end of the street, another column of mounted men advanced at the full gallop. They were a grim-faced bunch, were also heavily armed, but they wore no sort of masks.

'Better scared than a corpse, fellers,' Eady joined in. 'It's the deputies, an' it looks like they brought help.'

25

LAST LINE OF REASON

For many more minutes, a scene of terrifying disorder reigned – the savage shooting and yelling of the combatants, the snorting and screaming of the wounded horses. The cordite fumes made breathing difficult, stung nostrils and mouths as it was breathed in.

'Rufus!' Eady suddenly shouted and pointed. She was watching a hooded man who was giving orders. 'Recognize the roan? It's him, Rufe, an' he's turnin' for us.'

The man swung his mount towards Rufus and Eady, ran at them recklessly, as though it was his destiny. His gun roared, and Rufus felt a bullet thump the air as it went past his neck. The rider continued firing as he closed on Eady, but it was too late, he was taking bullets from both Rufus and Eady's guns. 'Killer bitch', he screamed, as he lost control of the roan.

The horse pulled up when it felt the sudden drag of the saddle horn, when a walnut-stocked shotgun clattered to the ground.

'I should have taken you when I had the chance – there's been a few,' the rider gasped, as he fell across the boardwalk at Eady's feet. 'Shouldn't have been so goddamn mealy-mouthed about it.'

'Yeah, that's real gallant,' Eady said, taking a stab at the man's dilemma. 'An' now I'm treadin' *your* nasty tail.'

In the street, the gunfire was more sporadic. The living Rosados, those not too badly wounded, were throwing down their guns and surrendering.

Assisted by the ranchers and their waddies, the townsfolk went into action. Within a few minutes, the street was clearing of smoke, and dead bodies and wreckage from the barricade was being carted away. The deputies dispatched new order, hauled five Rosados off to the jail.

'Rope corral 'em out back, if you have to,' Arnold called out.

Not wanting to spoil the occasion for themselves or anyone else, Rufus and Eady took an arm apiece and dragged the Rosado leader back across the street, down to the Tall Top saloon.

Already there were Wheat Cater, Emile Rednapp, Lyman Hench and Clovis Finn.

'We got ourselves a long day's celebratin' to do,' Cater announced. 'There's some been takin' bets on who it is you got there.'

'Strip him down to his black heart,' Hench rasped.

Rufus pulled at the juice-stained hood that covered the head of the fatally wounded outlaw. Startled growls and curses came from the men gathered around, as first the grizzled chin, then the dark-rooted teeth appeared in the hoary face of Pentland Betts.

'Jeeesus!' Arnold exclaimed in the outburst. 'An' there's me thinkin' the man shovelled horse-hockey for a livin'.'

'That's what we all thought,' Cater said, with a disgusted voice.

Betts glared evilly at the men surrounding him. 'Don't judge a man by his choice o' chaw,' he croaked.

'It was *you* killed Ida Rose, was it?' Eady demanded.

'An' Speke Dancer?' Rednapp wanted to know.

'Yeah . . . left that pretty little trimmin' on him . . . made you think about Rose comin' back . . . makin' up your own crackpot stories. But she coulda worked it out . . . you did. I killed her twice . . . had to.' Then Betts's pale, watery eyes squeezed up tight.

Eady turned away to look hard at Rufus. 'Shame that Ida couldn't have seen him now,' she said. 'Had you figured out who he was, Rufe?'

Rufus kept his eyes on Betts's face. He wanted the

154

man's eyes to open again, to see the expression of anger or bitterness. 'It was the shotgun,' he said. 'It's a break-action, English make. Not the sort a livery-man carries. An' we saw the roan when we hired them ol' duns. Not so long back when we came out o' the livery, you said you could almost smell him. Well, you *could*, Eady, an' we should have put it all together.'

Cater raised his head, then nodded very slowly. 'After the event, but it's all makin' sense now. An' the man was too obligin' by half.'

'Was it *him* planted the note an' money in your saddle pocket?' Eady said.

'Yeah, him or Greensleeves. But it was *his* idea.'

Betts's eyes opened, flicked like a lizard's from one to the other, as they all imagined and speculated.

'Tell me about Frimley,' The sheriff came close, lowered his head. '*Tell me*,' he menaced.

'We had it planned good. Goin' to buy death estates ... cheap. Railroad's runnin' a spur line across what woulda been our land. Would have been rich ... El Dorado.'

Rufus looked at Eady, nodded perceptively. Lyman Hench leaned in to speak to Betts.

'My cousin's got a spread close to the border,' the ranch owner said. 'He tells me the Topeka an' Santa Fe ain't runnin' anythin' out of Albuquerque, other than the track to Los Angeles. There ain't enough financial gain for 'em. They changed their mind, Betts. *There ain't no spur line.*'

The first signs of failure and hopelessness

wrenched at the corners of Betts's eyes, twisted his mouth.

Clovis Finn pushed on with the pent-up hostility. His words were angry and vehement. 'Good folk been dyin' for your stupid, useless greed, Betts. What's happenin' here ain't fit justice.'

Eady turned away from looking down at Betts. 'Did you ever speak to the night clerk . . . find out why he thought Speke Dancer weren't at the Longfield?' she asked Arnold.

'Yeah. He found the room key on the desk. Assumed he'd left without tellin' anybody. Simple mistake . . . nothin' more.'

'Lettin' me die makes none o' you any better.' Betts's face was pain-filled, ashen, and beaded with sweat. 'Get me the doc,' he groaned.

'How you goin' to pay, Betts? Suddenly, you ain't got a pot to piss in,' Arnold said coldly.

Now Emile Rednapp got across his thinking. 'One o' my men found Stub Jessel's body out by the wagon road,' he said. 'I ain't sheddin' a tear, but what did *he* do to Betts?'

'Don't know. Maybe we'll never know. But it was *me* who shot him,' Rufus said. 'Jessel was the one too many turkeys who pulled a gun on me. I gave him the chance to ride. He never took it.'

Arnold gave Rufus a doubtful look. 'Sometime, we'll have to talk that through,' he suggested. 'In the meantime, someone's got to haul this rubbish out to the one-mile limit.'

'Why not take him back to the livery? Shut the

door an' leave him there,' Eady said impassively.

'Yeah, 'cause he won't be needin' any pill roller,' Clovis Finn said, and dragged the hood back over Betts's lifeless features.

26

THE SETTLE DOWN

In the Longfield's dining-room, the doctor and the townswomen had finished most of their work with the wounded. Most of those helping out had returned home, and the lobby was no longer a waiting room for casualties. Along the street, a group of people had used buckets and bowls to empty the water troughs. They were sluicing down the boardwalks, tempering the dark pools of blood in the hard-packed dirt.

At the Tall Top saloon, Ogden Rimsayle approached a group of men who were sitting around a table that brimmed with Wheat Cater's best whiskey. The bank manager carried a puzzled expression across his jowly face as he turned to Rufus.

'You've admitted you *did* have money in your saddle-bags. That it was Betts or Greensleeves who planted it,' he said. 'Well, the deputies never got to findin' it, so I was wondering what happened.'

Rufus thought Rimsayle was an honest man, but

he didn't like him. He wanted to make him pay for his overbearing behaviour, because he'd been quick to accuse. 'It never existed. That was a touch o' short sweetenin' for the story,' he answered with a straight face. 'Makes you wonder if you an' Betts thought o' puttin' your own brand on them Denver bills.'

Rimsayle's eyes were popping with indignation. 'That's an imprecation,' he growled. 'Betts came to see me. He said he'd found the money in your saddle-bags – money that must have come from the Buchanan bank, and there was a note. And *that* ain't for sweetening any story, Mr Breese.'

'Yeeaah,' the sheriff contributed, with a look of amused incredulity. 'Kind o' curious, ain't it? But what gain did Betts have in concoctin' such windy, eh Rufus?'

'You'd have to ask *him* that. Wait for the resurrection,' Rufus chuckled.

Rimsayle tugged at the lapels of his frock coat. 'I was going to say that the town would have considered such an amount as recompense for your help, for the erroneous judgement of *some*,' he said with his dignity barely holding.

'Them words are as good as cash, Mr Rimsayle,' Rufus responded, with a broad, cynical smile. 'Me an' Eady are real appreciative.'

It was early morning, and in the mesquite and seep-willow trees along the Rio Gargara, Rufus and Eady once again sat their horses. But, this time, they were looking back at Quemadero.

Eady let her bayo mare drop its head to the water-side sedge. 'In spite of everythin', it *still* don't look the sort o' place that gives trouble,' she said.

'We been through this before,' Rufus explained. 'That's because we *ain't there*. A boneyard would be peaceable enough until we rode in.'

'Ha, that's very funny, Rufe,' Eady answered back. 'So what an' where's next? Seems the whole country's settlin' down ... goin' for the respectable and decent.'

'Yeah, well I'm thinkin' o' joinin' 'em, short order.'

'Aagh, why don't we go east? Take 'em some wild, natural habitat before it's lost. Show 'em it ain't *all* the stuff o' dime novels,' Eady suggested spiritedly.

'How'd we do that, for Chris'sake?'

'Well, Emile Rednapp thought we were a vaude-ville show. Maybe we could set up one o' them circuses. They're the newest thing, apparently.'

'It's an interestin' thought, Eady. We already got a couple o' routines.'

'Yeah, I know. We can get hold of a big ol' field tent from one o' the Texas fort sutlers.'

Rufus looked hard at Eady when she pressed him for how much he thought it would cost.

'Five hundred dollars should set us up,' he said, slow and thoughtful, the anticipation just nipping at him.

'That's what I thought.' Eady smiled, walked her horse forward through the peacefully running water. 'Maybe there'll be a few towns to trigger on the way.'